# AN-TAN-TIRI MOGODAN

# *An-Tan-Tiri Mogodan*

Short Stories

by

**FLORINA ENACHE**

Adelaide Books
New York / Lisbon
2019

AN-TAN-TIRI MOGODAN
Short Stories
By Florina Enache

Copyright © by Florina Enache
Cover design © 2019 Adelaide Books

Published by Adelaide Books, New York / Lisbon
adelaidebooks.org

Editor-in-Chief
Stevan V. Nikolic

For any information, please address Adelaide Books
at info@adelaidebooks.org

or write to:

Adelaide Books
244 Fifth Ave. Suite D27
New York, NY, 10001

ISBN-10: 1-951214-41-2
ISBN-13: 978-1-951214-41-8

Printed in the United States of America

*"Till we had nothing but thoughts and memories in common."*

*Ezra Pound, Exile's Letter*

# Contents

Three Days in the Life of a Translator   *9*

The New Man   *17*

You're in the Army Now   *29*

State I   *37*

An-Tan-Tiri Mogodan   *41*

Wedding   *69*

We Build the Country – the Country We Build   *77*

Mademoiselle   *89*

The Little Girl Has Curly Hair   *101*

Purity   *107*

Rite of Passage   *113*

But Deliver Us from Evil   *119*

*About the Author*   *125*

# Three Days in the Life of a Translator

## One

They knocked down houses to build apartment blocks. The dogs had nowhere to go. The city is full of stray dogs and battalions of rats. We are a nation that has nowhere to go. Nothing we see is ours. Up there it's warm with festooned garlands. Down here it's cold and filthy. Fear lingers in the air. Before the clouds. The air is bloated with applause. Forty years of applause had to go somewhere.

My feet beat the streets. Long streets I don't know the names of. Tall blocks united against the sky. In between the blocks, skeletal trees are ashamed. They could have been in a forest. They would die undignified and smothered by concrete. We could all have done better. The garbage chutes stink even in the winter. People have jars with pickles in them on their balconies, in the cold.

Winter is a hard test most humans fail. My feet are in close connection with nature. When it's cold, they let me know right away. When it rains, even sooner. The flats I am wearing outlived their functionality by four years. Their decency by five.

Today was warm for a winter day. Beggars and cripples came out of the ground like daffodils. Jesus lives in each one of them. Jesus wears rags. His skin is scruffy with dried-blood scars and frostbitten. Jesus has toothless mouths like black holes and oily hair with nests of lice in it, like diamond studs.

People on the subway wear the same face. From the underground, packs of them go to the bodega. They all search for something. A hand to hold theirs when it shakes. Wool cotton to stuff in their mouths. A whack across their heads. They wear parkas in inappropriate colours, as if they were all going skiing. I burrow into a yellow feather jacket. This jacket is the best thing that ever happened to me. In the footwear department, I fail.

I wait in line for thirty minutes. I no longer own my feet. They've got bread, people whisper. Yellow loaves dumped in plastic crates rest on the oily floor. They clean it with petrol. The woman cuts the bread and mounds of crumbs are left behind on the table. The woman looks at my card and says no, you are from the country. She gives me a hunk of halvah instead. She cuts it with the long knife and drops it in my hand in its oily paper. I can't put it in my bag. It would ruin my dictionary. I carry it in my hand and it greases my hand up to my elbow.

I rent a small apartment on the ground floor. It is colder inside than outside. An old man lived here, but he died recently. His family keeps his photo on the table. In front of it, there is a small candle I have to light every night. My wages cover the rent. For the bills, I borrow.

My feet carry me to my block. My feet shake harder the closer they get to the building. My feet are terrified. The rest of me is happy. Tonight, they give us hot water. In less than two minutes, I sink in hot water to warm up. My skin is red. My feet tingle. A tap on the window. I freeze in the hot water.

I'm glad you are taking a bath I might come to visit you later. I jump out and splash water on the floor and on the walls.

I rub my skin dry in a hurry to put clothes on. I want to turn off the light, but it is too late: he knows I am home. My mouth tastes metallic. A light knock at the door this time. Do you have a light? Then silence. I tremble. There is no escape. He lives upstairs with his brothers. They are not part of the working class. Mrs. Klein from across the hall tells me that a man in a dark suit brings them beer. Mrs. Klein has iron grills on her windows and the front door. She keeps them locked at all times. Get out of there, people at work said to me. One day they will rape you or kill you. Easy for them to say, but where to go?

## Two

This year the winter is poor. There is no snow. Just frozen dust. It goes up my nose and slaps my face. There is no blood in my face. In the morning, I reset my life to where it was yesterday. In the street, I see the same faces with bags under abandoned eyes. We are a nation that wakes up in the heart of the night to get a place in line to buy meat. Or toilet paper. The night we carry in our heads all day is as useless as the perfect lines in front of empty shops.

The sidewalk is slippery. My feet no longer listen to me. People go to work, buried in routine. They pass me. Not one looks at me. A stranger, seeing my ungainly dance, offers me his arm. He is tall and wears wonderful boots with thick soles that grip the ground. When we reach clean cement, he leaves me without a word.

I love my English dictionary and the Oxford companions. I have to use the technical dictionary every day. A group of engineers wrote it. They knew engineering. The director received a washing machine as a present. He asks me to translate the manual. He has rotten teeth and his suit is shiny from wear. I feel sorry for that suit, so close to his body.

The head of personnel wears a cable knit sweater. His sister sent it to him from Germany. His job is to preen the director. The head of personnel knows things about everybody. He is not a married man. He has an affair with the librarian. The library has big windows. When they fuck, they look out at the building where her husband works. He is a researcher. There is a lot of natural light in the library.

I report to a man who hasn't finished high school. He wears a suit and a white shirt every day. His job is to carry the director's briefcase. His own briefcase is black and square. His mother carefully puts his lunch inside it every morning. She is an activist. He buys the Party's central newspaper at the metro and reads it at work. His shirts are impeccable. One night he comes home with me to help me finish an urgent translation. He never studied English. Only Russian. When I come back from the kitchen, his pants are neatly folded on the back of a chair. His moustache is wiry and smells of soup. My bed is lumpy and I wear too many clothes. His hands know what they want, but my legs are stubborn. He guides me to him. He begs. He shuts the bathroom door too hard. I listen to the rattle of his wrist chain. I stare at the spot on the floor where his square briefcase has been. I want to ignore the hot patch like the mouth of a volcano. Shame paints my face red. The heat spreads inside me like a balm.

Big foreign delegation announced for today. Tell the translator to wear something decent, for Christ's sake. The director dislikes my wardrobe. I should be more glamourous. There is no glamour in the wage he pays me. Woollen sweater will choke the smell of sweat when deodorant is not an option.

Consultants. They come to give us funding. They wear petrol-grey suits and plaster smiles. They are cautious and polite. They believe a translator is there to provide them with services. If you make a mistake, they smile. They will tell you how to translate numbers, later, in their hotel room, after they fucked you, for free. They promise to bring you a good dictionary when they come next time. There is no next time. Plaster smile.

After the meeting, they get friendly. There is food on the table. They allow me to stay. They ask me what I do with my tongue when I speak English. They don't expect an answer. The director laughs. The others laugh. I believe the languages we know, somewhere in our heads, hold hands and dance the hora. I keep silent. My lips are not trained in the lie of smiling. The director's feet don't get along with his guts. They play hide-and-seek. He wobbles toward me. He stacks his body on the chair next to mine. There is beer on his breath and garlic. You have no idea how much I wanna fuck you. He pushes his tongue into my right ear. It's slimy and hot. I tilt my head to the left. There is grease on his chin and part of a lettuce leaf is stuck on it. A snail hand crawls between my legs. I scrape back my chair and bolt. You don't like a national dick, ha? The garlic smell hits the back of my head. You only want to be fucked in English, ha? I'll give you my balls to translate them. You fucking bitch. You will be fucking sorry. He turns to the director of personnel. She will be sorry. The director's lips twist. His head is heavy. It plonks on the table into scraps of roast beef, fish and garlic aioli, chicken in aspic.

Today I got paid and borrowed some money. My feet are happy. The new boots have fur inside and long laces. My new boots are fit to climb mountains. The Cinemathequé is in an old building, but inside I see people with long hair who are not hollow. The furniture is musty and the wooden floors creak. I dream about being the soul of this place. To live in the old chairs, in the old velvet curtain, in the tiny translator's booth. My body would be the small tickets people hold in their hands. I would be the faces magnified on the screen. I would be Cleopatra, or Lawrence of Arabia, or Victor Laszlo. Tonight, I would be Cabiria, the sad prostitute who seeks true love. I would cry because, yet again, I have been deceived, but life is beautiful and there is always circus. Clowns, hula hoopers, and jugglers. My tears would wet the wide screen already yellowed by time. Usually, when the movie is over, I have to go back into my body. In the reality outside, a higher authority powders snow from above. Oblivious flakes swirl where a cathedral has been, filling the void left behind by bulldozers. Snow muffles pain and poverty but covers it all.

I beat the streets with my tired feet. I want to never arrive anywhere. I want to never stop. My feet know the way. They carry me to my block. My feet shake harder the closer they get to the building. My feet are terrified.

## Three

I come to work in the morning. February is a difficult month. There is a small square room at the gate. It is the office for the day guard and a house for the night guard. The night guard sleeps there and heats his baked beans. A blue-and-mustard blanket covers a table he uses as a bed. A green plant wouldn't survive in here. The day guard hands me an envelope. The head of personnel has written my name on it. The day guard insists that I read it right away. His stomach is big and it blocks the door. They say, if a person is fat, the file is thin. If the person is thin, the file is fat. I read and the words 'dismissed for incompetence' stick to my tongue like a lump. I can't spit it out or swallow it. My feet turn me around as if I were a robot. I head to the subway. A new page will be added to my file today.

The carriage is empty. I sit down. I unzip my jacket. Yellow lights swish by. The train whispers something but the words chew each other. My mind fights to breathe but it drowns. I clutch the bag to my chest. The hard cover of the dictionary prods through my clothes. Someone said in school, the dictionary is a lifesaver for any translator. My head is round like a football. It doesn't fit into corners. It bounces on the hard plastic chairs. Some are yellow or blue. Most of them are red.

# *The New Man*

He lives with the others, all locked up in a cell as big as a country. There are no walls to stop anyone, but the reality is all the worse because it has the appearance of freedom. Every day, they all spew out in the streets from the apartment blocks and maintain the illusion of living in a perfectly normal city, in a perfectly normal country.

Every day he beats the streets with stoicism and regularity of a duty. Out in the cold, you don't belong. Out in the cold, you think you are free. Almost the same route every day, around the university, the museum, the Athenaeum, the Victory Boulevard. He learned the patches of broken asphalt, the potholes, the piles of garbage, the smallpox-eaten walls of old buildings, the dark corners full of human excrements, the beggars and their lairs, the barbed wire.

The city still bears the scars of the March 1977 earthquake and the newspapers and the two-hour-per night TV program still talk about the heroes who successfully survived under the ruins for weeks, without any water or food. New constructions quickly replaced the historic buildings and they popped up like mushrooms after the rain, but his mind, swaddled in memories, rejects the new ones and stubbornly rewinds the black-and-white images of the time before, like a movie projected on a yellowed bedsheet.

He boosts up his shoulders to resist the cold, to expand his body, to occupy some space, to count as a human being, to have thoughts and feelings. He feels he is nobody, a middle-aged man in a dark suit and a grey overcoat, a regular shadow on a canvas of indifferent streets in a cold city.

The dust is carried by the wind and it gives its colour: grey. Darkness pounces over the city like a heavy blanket. Old cars with struggling engines crawl past. Lesser people, men and women, with almost no physical body in their old clothes, trudge by. They carry in their hands plastic bags that read Marlboro or Aldi or Wrangler Jeans, always empty.

This is long after the leaves have fallen.

He glances behind. The interior of the station is always the same, with railway lines and long straight platforms. It was a warm summer day, back then, many years ago, but it feels like yesterday. A gypsy woman, dipped in yellow and pink and green, with gleams of gold in her hair, was selling flowers on the platform and he bought a bunch of mums for Hanna, it was almost autumn. The pavement was wet and the heat radiated through his tennis shoes. He was young and free and the sun was playing in his hair.

When he could no longer see the train, eaten by distance, he could still feel it inside him, as it moved away, choking his throat and burning inside his eyes. She never came back. And then they shut the gates. That day, every step on the wet pavement brought him closer to his loneliness. Day after day, he lost himself. After a while, a number of years, he smashed the frail frame of self-deception and plunged into an automatic life led by a compulsory magnetism and enrolled in anonymity, like all the others.

He was tired. It was over. It still is.

Like every other morning, his steps carry him up the large worn-out stairs of the university building. He struggles to get excited. Sometimes, he succeeds. Behind the massive wood doors, students rush to and from their classes or they gather in small clusters to talk and laugh, their young faces unclouded. They greet him with a smile. He is *the Prof.* They all read his books and course texts and they fill up the amphitheatre to its capacity to hear him speak. He is loved here.

The cold in room 101 on the ground floor can only compete with the one outside, courtesy of the large old drafty windows. But they are all here, waiting. It is the English Literature workshop. Today they discuss Hemingway's *The Short Happy Life of Francis Macomber*. He finds it ironic that Hemingway has passed the censorship claws more due to a certain friendship than to his literary merit. He thinks that someone above made a simplistic judgement but, all the same, it is the students' gain to study him and he loves it and it makes him even happier to see that his students love it, too. It is their ration of freedom.

It is a story about courage. It is a story about a rich American man who went to Africa, on a safari, to prove to his trophy wife, that he is worth something. It is clear they have read the full story. They must have taken turns in the freezing library to read it. And he knows there is only one copy of the *Short Stories*.

They talk about Africa and safari with wide-open eyes and confidence, as if they went there. They consider the plot, the narrative, the characters, the symbols and the subtle meanings. They feel sorry for Francis as he gets to be a man but for such a short time. They swirl the 'r' in the dome of their mouths, as they heard in the few American movies allowed to the public and not dubbed.

The girl who chopped her hair when she got lice in the dorm, feels sorry for the animals to be hunted and killed for no reason. The lion and the buffalo are 'good' animals, she quotes, why kill them? Francis is a rabbit, Margot is a lion and Wilson, the professional hunter, is a hyena. They laugh.

A boy quotes their own Emil Cioran. *A world without tyrants would be as annoying as a zoo without hyenas.* He says the words and there is silence. Cioran, the philosopher, the prophet, has defected. He lives in Paris. They hear their own breathing. Only their eyes dart nervously throughout the room without meeting other eyes.

The cold has become disrespectful. They hide their hands in pockets, or under the trim of their sweaters or cross their arms and cradle their hands underneath.

A boy with curly hair like a brush thinks that Wilson is wise; he understands the world better than the rich people he serves for money. The principle he lives by, in his own words, from Shakespeare, is 'damned good:' *By my troth, I care not; a man can die but once; we owe God a death and let it go each way it will he that dies this year is quit for the next.* They all take a moment to think about this. They look impressed and a few shadows pass about their young faces.

He embraces them all with his eyes, with the arms of his soul, taking in this moment and the feeling that fills up his heart.

Outside, metallic clouds huddle toward the East. The buildings are dirty, wet with rain. The wind hits him in the face.

At night, insomnia sticks needles in his eyes. He lies in bed immobile as if paralysed. He pulls down his eyelids and sees

Hanna, drenched in sunshine, running through a house full of light, with open windows and white curtains swelled by the breeze from the sea. The multitude and freedom of waves.

He pulls the covers over his head and lets them sag on his face, like a death mask.

In the morning, he sticks a different mask to his face, one made of indifference. The mornings are all the same, grilled by his wife, he must pull his weight and live up to the expectations. He escapes the big house through the back. He catches a glimpse of himself in a window at the metro station: he does not look the way he feels but much older, dressed in clothes bought by his wife.

He was familiar with this part of the city, at some point. As a student, he came here a lot to visit his colleagues who lived in the hostels, but that was a long time ago, maybe twenty years. The hostels are all gone now and, instead, there are factories and huge hangars rising boldly against the sky, thick industrial towers belching out smoke and gas and from, time to time, flames.

He remembers those times when he used to visit Hanna. The few moments spent alone with her at the garbage chute, the stolen kisses and hot embraces and the sighs. He hasn't been thinking about Hanna for a long time. Too painful. And her memory begins to fade. He is getting old.

He was sent to attend this course about the creation of the New Man, as part of the compulsory academic training. Maybe he is late, he thinks, but he doesn't check his watch. He advances slowly and hesitantly, shuffling his legs. He can see his own breath billowing from his mouth, in front of his face. A tentative of rain swings by, blasted by the wind. He has no umbrella.

He thinks the smell of earth, freshly-dug earth, not the one when you dig a grave, but the one when you work in the garden and you plant bulbs, in early spring, with dry seeds rustling in your hand and, above you, the continuous whisper of leaves, high and green, and a crisp wind ruffles your hair and makes you realise you are alive.

There is heavy noise and rattle of bulldozers from a construction site. A forest of cranes carves into the sky. He learned there is nothing behind that sky. Steel frames and concrete blocks await their turn, stacked on the ground. There is rubble and mud spilling out on the streets. The wind carries cement dust. He feels the grit in his teeth and in his eyes. His shoes stick to the fresh tar and hot steam burns his skin through his pants. The wind, in its fury, tortures the few leafless trees left uncut.

At this time of the year, everything must die. Some, for ever.

His eyes land on the building from afar. It is a tall and wide construction, with green wire-meshed windows, neatly aligned, twelve on each storey and twelve storeys up. Inside, there are wood panels on the walls in the lobby and green linoleum covers the heavy chlorinated floors. Identical white doors line up the corridors on both sides. Only the numbers nailed close to the top are different.

The classroom is large and warm, with dirty light from outside sieved through the wire-meshed windows, four of them. He signs the standard personal declaration and, with his eyes down, strides straight to a spare desk. He sits and braces himself for a full day of propaganda. The teacher speaks at large about the national myths and the correct political direction, as an introduction to the subject at hand. The future will be grandiose and at all possible due to the rebirth of the New Man. The teacher knows the text by heart and speaks it ceremoniously, with eyes shut and straight body, as if standing at attention.

He herds his thoughts in and locks them away. He empties his head. He does his best to focus on the course. To memorise something to remember at the end in case they ask questions. His eyelids bang shut and it is dark; they spring open and he tangles in a woman's hair, blond and sunny, in contrast with the grim weather outside. He follows the straight line of her back sloping down into her waist, just to flare up again into her round hips. She turns her head and smiles at him. He looks away, embarrassed he's been caught and disappointed with her cherry lipstick.

During recess, he leaves the room to find a place to smoke. There is a balcony at the end of the corridor, where the garbage chute is. He finds the blond woman there smoking. Seeing her makes him happy, although he can't explain why. He asks her for a light. He sheaths the lighter in her hand with his both hands, big and warm, against the wind. His eyes flicker over the chipped polish on her fingernails to her face and lips. She smokes national unfiltered cigarettes and she keeps picking up threads of tobacco from her lips.

"My name is Lilli," she says and smiles.

"Paul. Nice to meet you."

They smoke in silence. The wind shakes the loose balustrade causing a threatening rattle. The door glass is missing and the wind travels freely through the long corridor with great force.

Lilli is shivering in her thin coat. Paul feels he should hug her, to protect her against the wind or anything else. She feels his eyes on her and her hands are shaking visibly.

"I live around the corner," she says, suddenly. "Would you like to come for a coffee? Later?" Her gaze is calm, only her lips twitch slightly.

He is caught off-guard, but he says quickly, "Yes, I would love to."

Back in the classroom, it is even more impossible than before for him to focus. He imagines her place, an apartment, most likely, in this part of the city. He is nervous, he has never done this before, and excited. His clothes are close to his skin.

They grab the brown paper bags, the lunch, and rush out. She takes him around the building, through the back into a street unknown to him, two strangers walking side by side, unsynchronised, not knowing what to say. He has turned inside himself, what is he doing? He is a married man. He has no answer. He doesn't feel any guilt, just cold.

Lilli's hand, small and nervous, insinuates itself in between his elbow and his body. The gesture brings him back to this moment, now and here, with this girl. They are going to her place to have sex when they should be in class learning about the rebirth of the New Man. He lets her hand squeeze in and stares down at her face. Whipped by the wind, it is rosy and young, with tight skin and sweet lines. She smiles because she is nervous. "It's not far," she said embarrassed, feeling his eyes on her again.

A few moments later, her hand twitches like a little sparrow under his arm. "It's here, in the basement." She climbs down a few steps. He follows obediently and carefully, trying to squish his body into the narrow space, then through a dark corridor. "Sorry, the light is broken." She grabs his hand in the dark with unexpected familiarity and he follows her easily, their steps whispers on the wet floor. She unlocks a door and enters.

A strong smell of mould chokes him. The room is quite small and filled with old furniture. A huge wardrobe with its doors hanging half-open covers almost the whole wall. Inside it, old dresses and fur coats hang crammed together; velvet and lace and silk swabbed with the sweat and dreams of a defunct world. On a decrepit dresser, somebody has placed the black-and-white photo of an old woman, like the ones you see on the marble crosses in the graveyard, and a candle in front of it, like an altar. The wide bedhead has chubby cherubs in its woodwork, but the mattress is lumpy and covered with a cheap blanket depicting the *Abduction from the Seraglio*.

Paul looks around, undecided, and his heart sinks a little. He thinks he can hear the moths eat the ancient fabrics in the wardrobe and feels oppressed by the pungent smell and the low ceiling. There is a small window higher on the wall through which he hears noises from the street: the clattering tram, the few cars and a handful of defeated passers-by. Filthy light filters through the window, maybe because the window is dirty, as she cannot reach to clean it, or maybe because outside the day is running away from the streets, leaving behind darkness and mud.

"Sorry for the room. An old woman died and the family let me live here for a while. I am paying rent." Then silence. "Are you cold?" she asks rubbing her hands. "They don't give us heat before the first of December, but I can borrow a portable from my neighbour upstairs, if you want."

"I am okay," he says but he is obviously cold. "Do you really have coffee?" he asks again to make conversation.

"No, not really. This is what people say for this kind of thing, I mean, for sex."

"Yes, you are right," he tries to smile.

He sits down on one of the two ancient chairs set next to an even more ancient table covered in yellowed lace. He is embarrassed. He has no idea what to do next. He pulls out his cigarette pack. "May I?"

"Sure," she nods. She hangs her coat on a nail on the back of the door. With trembling fingers, she unbuttons her shirt, takes it off and places it carefully on the back of the other chair. She takes off her bra and covers her small breasts with her hands as if she were shy or cold. She pulls down the tight skirt and sets it neatly with the shirt.

Burrowed in his overcoat, he is watching her, smoking and almost forgetting to breathe.

She wears black nylons up mid-thigh, clasped in black suspenders hooked to a garter belt. She slips down her panties but keeps the nylons. Her panties, shaped like a flower, rest on the top of her clothes. He stares through a curtain of smoke at the black triangle between her legs. She is ready now and she lies face-up on the bed. Her right arm goes up and behind her head. Her breasts are smooth and round, the size of green apples in the spring before they ripen. He could fit one in each palm. She spreads her legs slightly and raises her knees. "Are you going to sit there?"

A wave of warmth crosses his body. Only a crimson rash on his neck betrays him. He butts the cigarette on a dirty plate left on the table. He takes off his shoes and hangs the overcoat on the nail hugging hers. He takes off his jacket, then the pants and the tie. He keeps the socks. He treads lightly to the bed, two steps only, very close. He removes his jocks and throws them on his chair and kneels on the bed, between her legs.

He smothers her tiny body with his, her nylons still on, his shirt still on. She is nimble with her hands and hips and guides him. He obeys and enjoys it. "You'll have to excuse me," he whispers in her ear, "I might be too quick. It's been a long time. My wife. She's an activist." Her hand cups the nape of his neck. "It's okay," she says and kisses him deep on the mouth.

The room is no longer cold but still musty. She lies naked under a quilt with no sheet, smoking one of his cigarettes. He wipes himself with an old towel somebody else has used before. He puts his jocks back on, sits on a chair and lights a cigarette. He feels a lot better now.

"Where do you work?" she asks.

"I teach at the university. You?"

"I work at the textile factory. I am in Exports." She tries to make it sound important.

"You are very nice," he adds and, right away, he regrets it because he doesn't want to make any promises.

"Thank you. You are nice, too."

"We should go back," he says and butts his cigarette. Then he changes his mind and says, "Could I ask you a favour? I hope it's okay, but it's been a long time for me. Do you mind if we -? Can we do it again? Is that all right with you?"

She is still lying under the quilt. She glances at him. Her chin juts up and a big laugh bursts out. He could see all her teeth, like a string of white pearls. "You are so sweet. Of course."

She comes and takes his hand and walks with him to the bed. She pulls his shirt over his head and kisses his chest in little pecks, touching him only lightly, almost not touching at all. They lie down on the bed, next to each other. His fingers unclasp and roll down her nylons, thin as a whisper, and his lips heal the marks on her skin.

His hands are clumsy but they hunger to learn her body, the secret places, the soft lines of her breasts and hips, the ascending curve of her inner thighs, the buttons of her spine like a string of beads, elusive under her skin, the delicate down under her arms and on her pubis, the soft arch of her upper lip, her quiver when he kisses her neck and wiggles his tongue inside her ear.

He has never been so close to a woman before. His body yearns to learn the mystery of another body, unknown to him and yet so familiar; another human being that is lovely and soft and good. He knows what to do this time and she abandons herself to him and he drowns himself in her.

Something gets loose in his chest and all the love he carried for Hanna over the years, all of it, pours out into this girl and he sobs and moves in a rhythm he never knew he had in him, and his hands grapple her body too hard, like a man who drowns and fights to save his own life and maybe hers, too, and a snowdrop of fear in her eyes tells him he could hurt her and he should stop, but her touch brands his skin and he is dizzy with the smell of her and his body wants to be insider hers and engulf hers, at the same time, and all that has been wrong in his life is good now and he is freed of pain and his salty tears drop on her lips and she kisses his eyes and cups the nape of his neck with her both hands.

She comes back to him as he is sitting on the bed, naked and not ashamed, feeling relaxed and a bit sticky. She hands him his brown bag, the lunch. She tears up hers and reveals a bread roll and a cube of cheese. The bread is fresh and she sinks her teeth in it with an embarrassed smile, she is hungry. He smiles at her and they both eat bread and cheese, sitting naked on the lumpy bed.

The cold can no longer touch them.

Outside, snow is starting to drift in small flakes from the leaden sky, settling onto the grey buildings and the grey street and the grey people.

# You're in the Army Now

We moved from the mouth of hell to its ass. At the end of our first university year, we complete compulsory military training. We moved from the squalid hostel to the military barracks. The room has peeling walls and stained lino that rolls back. Metallic bunks are stacked on top of each other. There is dried blood and urine on the mattresses. There is mould in the corners and obscene writings on the walls. A windowpane is missing. Somebody has pinned a blue plastic bag in its place. There are no curtains. The three of us share a room with three girls from Horticulture.

In the morning, we go to the military headquarters. We have to be there before seven. The uniform has to be impeccably pressed and clean. My boots are too big and the belt has a metallic buckle that digs into my flesh. I have shoved my hair under the cap. I am not presentable. The day promises to heat up. In the military grounds, grey buildings sprawl on the grass. The few trees around are tired and covered in dust.

We gather on the assembly ground between the administration building and the materiel building. We fall in by faculty, standing at attention. We salute the major who is in charge of us all. We keep standing at attention. We pledge allegiance to the flag of the country, its supreme commandant and the blood of our heroes. The major speaks about the honour of being in the army, the true military spirit and the three principles we follow: obedience, hard work and courage. The major has a big ass to mark her place in the world and in the military hierarchy.

The major walks along the ranks. She stops in front of our platoon. We are standing at attention looking straight in front of us. We are not breathing. We sweat but we stand rigid. Our heels together, our palms sweating along our tights. One cadet from Humanities is missing, she says. We freeze. Do you know why? Her eyes drill into us. She smirks. Because she is having an abortion today. Silence as thick as the dust in the air. How do we know? Because we know everything. Yes, everything, she says. We breathe in the dust. We dare not cough. I can promise you, I will bring her here and I will personally dishonour her. I will rip off her insignia and throw it in the dust. Under the wheels of the tanks. She is dead for us. Army is discipline above everything.

We are still in the ranks marching towards the fields. The road is unpaved and the boots stir the dust. The gun I carry, 1969 model, crushes the bones in my right shoulder. The kaki bag I am wearing cross body is heavy with military equipment. I have a shovel clasped to my duty belt in the back. The sun doesn't forgive. The captain wears sunglasses under the visor of her officer hat. There are red patches on her cheeks. She puffed her boobs out and she walks along the front end of the platoon where the girls from Horticulture march. Humanities are in the back.

The heat has burnt the grass. The few straws that still stand up are dead. There are wooden targets at the far end of the field. Cadets and soldiers use them equally. The latrines are not far from the targets. The women's latrines have no doors. A few scruffy trees give the hope of shade. The captain orders us to halt just before we reach the shade. My body is sinking under the weight of military equipment. The sun burns my face and the small triangle at the base of my neck. My blood pounds in my temples and blocks my ears.

Horticulture, at ease, she says. Go and sit in the shade. Now, Humanities, I have something special for you today. I will make you pay for your colleague who has the abortion. You will have to suffer. That's the rule in the army. Do you see that hill over there? Her finger points at a mound at the far side of the field. Yes, captain, we say. That's the objective, she says. I want you to get there as soon as you possibly can. Run. Fast. When you get there, I want you to run back as fast as you can. Understood? And, by the way, from now on, don't use aspirin as birth control even if you hold it tight between your knees. It doesn't work. She laughs. Horticulture laugh with her.

They started running, in broken ranks, in complete disorder, in scattered bunches of tiny khaki soldiers crushed down by clattering equipment, their untrained bodies smothered by thick woollen uniforms. Their faces were purple and their open mouths were gulping hot air. The veins in their necks were swollen and their bodies were drenched in sweat. They closed their eyes and wanted to die.

Somebody somewhere must be protecting us. We make it all the way back. My uniform is wet. The skin inside my boots has teamed up with the socks. Blisters as big as egg yellows puddle on my heels. We are in the ranks again for inspection. I look down. Blood pours down from my nose. My knees give in. I collapse. On my way down, I bump my head on the gun in front of me. I am too close. My friend Sylva leaves her place and jumps to me. She holds my face in her hands. Her hands tremble. The captain is inches from us. The tip of her right boot has an itch for my ribs and liver. It has to bite the dust. This time. Stand up, she says. I obey. *Don't cry.* Don't give this bitch that satisfaction, stand up straight, don't tremble, show her what Humanities are made of. You are a disgrace, she says. Look at you, all covered in blood. You soiled the uniform. You are not worthy enough to wear this uniform.

A platoon of soldiers with their lieutenant becomes visible on the other side of the scarce trees. Soldiers see girls. They whistle. The red patches on the captain's face are redder than usual. She orders the Humanities to stand at attention. She walks over to the soldiers. The lieutenant comes in front to meet her. They move toward the scrub, a few meters away from the soldiers. He speaks in a low voice. She giggles. We know what's coming next. I turn the other way. I unsling the gun. We all do. We slump in the dried grass, in between dry manure and scars from military exercises. The sun is above. Flies buzz around trying to get into our eyes and mouths. We hear her pant and moan. We hear the soldiers root for their lieutenant. Then he zips up and lights a cigarette. The smoke hangs low in the thick air.

She comes back to us, all read in the face and sweaty. Wet patches darken her kaki shirt between her breasts and at her armpits. We stand at attention. I have a new exercise for you, she says. She is calmer and looks exhausted. I want you to file in two lines, Horticulture and Humanities, face-to-face. Now, Horticulture will spit on Humanities. What do Humanities do? Nothing. This exercise is called *spitting on Humanities.*

I close my eyes and fold my lips into my mouth. I stick my chin into my neck. The girl in front of me lifts up my chin with her hand. She blasts her load on my right cheek and eye. She has eaten garlic and smoked. I am going to throw up. *Don't cry.*

The shortest girl in Humanities has no pair. She is the shortest so she carries the hardtack. There is no hardtack today. So there is nobody to spit on you, the captain says. The shortest girl tries to smile. Her smile is tortured. Her uniform is too big. She is our colleague and she wrote the dictionary. You know what we are going to do? The captain asks, but it is not a real question. Humanities will spit on their own colleague, we hear. Understood? There are stones in her voice and they hit us in the face. We don't move. Are you deaf or just plain stupid? She is furious now. There is no place for sentimentalism in the army. Get on with it. We file in and, one-by-one, we spit on the girl who wrote the dictionary.

We are dismissed. We find our own way back to the barracks. Sylva and I cut through the park. The park is empty. A man in his forties with his baby boy sits on a bench. Sylva speaks to the baby. He puts his little arms out to her. Come with us, Sylva says. The father says, why don't you come with us? We live close by and we have a car. I will fuck you both. You first, while your friend watches the baby, then I fuck her. What do you say? We say nothing. We turn around and go. The trees have knitted their branches above in a cathedral.

The bear in the cage is tap dancing. His ribs poke through the sparse fur that hangs in dirty tufts. He used to be a circus bear, the park worker tells us. He is too old now, that's why he ended up here. Sylva asks, do you know they teach them to dance by making them walk on a hot surface? The bear on the hot tin roof? She looks at me, yes, something like that.

We come back from the mess hall. We are hungry. In the army soup, the carrots still have dirt on them. I break the bread and a worm plunges in my soup. Worms have nutritional value, we are told. I save a heel of bread for Mara, our roommate. We go back to the room. We climb the stairs. I am still hungry. I am angry. I hurl the bread at the window. The window cracks. Like a river on the map of Eastern Europe. In front of our door, my heart pounds in my mouth. My hand on the handle doesn't listen. Sylva pushes me, come on, she is okay, you'll see.

She looks dead. Her lips are the colour of lavender. Her face has borrowed the hue of the dirty walls. She opens her eyes when I touch her shoulder. She doesn't know what to-morrow will bring. They are coming for her. Her irises, moss green speckled with gold, try to escape her eyes. She is dou-bled up on the dirty mattress. Her bunk is under one of the three Horticulture girls. Right now, they are cooking eggs on the ironing machine. The smoke chokes the room. A blanket covers the window.

The water in the shower stabs daggers into my head. I have to wash. I stink. The door opens and Mara jumps in the narrow box. I don't have time to say a word. Her body sticks to mine under the puny jet. Don't turn off the water. She whispers, please help me. I can't do it alone. She looks sick. We shiver. Our teeth chatter. We'll help you, I say. I'll talk to Sylva. She kisses me. There is death in her kiss. I hold her tight. She is skin-and-bones. We both are.

We don't have toilet paper. We use the pages of an old notebook. I write on one and place it under the others. I go back into the room and tell Sylva to go to the toilet. She eyes me curiously but she goes. She comes back and winks. Her hair covers the sides of her face.

Memories of things never happened visit me in my sleep. To-night I dream of steamy cups of coffee. Sylva's hand grazes my shoulder. It's time to go, her eyes tell me in the dark. I wear my jeans to be safe. I have two red lips on my T-shirt and a big tongue. I saved hard for my T-shirt. We slip out in the corridor towards the garbage chute. The yellow light is dim and we can't see much. I tuck the flip-flops in my back pockets. There are puddles on the cement floor. I step on rat carcasses. My toes meet their downy bodies and crush their bones. The ones still alive scurry away. We clamber down the stairs. I clutch the sticky bannister and hold Mara by her shoulders.

A shape moves in the stench around the chute. I say to Sylva, someone's here. It's Rita, Mara says. She has my baby girl. The woman hands Mara a shoebox and says, God rest her little soul. Rita is a big woman who lives in the garbage behind the barracks. Many men have met Rita in the dark, but they don't remember her in the daylight.

We cut through the back of the barracks, across the grass field. We run. Mara is weak. She doesn't let go of the shoe box. We sneak out through the hole in the wall. There is no wind. The moon is turned off. We are dressed in darkness. There is light somewhere else. A train whistles far away. A narrow path between abandoned buildings. A thought carries me to our mothers and fathers. They live far away with big fists in their mouths. I hear a thump behind. A bitter taste rises in my mouth. *Don't look back.* Stray dogs raise their heads. They are too weak to bark. They are tamed by hunger. We cross train tracks. The gravel sticks into the soles of my flip-flops. I look back. *I feel somebody is watching.*

The whole vast plateau looked deserted. There was no grass growing there anymore. Only scruffy brambles and milk thistles lived in hostile harmony. The ground was hard and unfriendly. When it rained, the place was full of mud and puddles. The garbage dumped there over the years, regularly ravaged by scavenging birds and dogs, and scoured by gypsies for scrap metal and food, turned into mountains, valleys and hills. There was talk about building an Olympic stadium on this land. Old people say there was a Jewish cemetery there once. They still remember the morning when the bulldozers trampled down the monuments and levelled out the dirt. White bones stuck out like stems of lilies.

We dig the ground with spoons we stole from the mess hall. The ground is stubborn. It hasn't rained for a long time. Juicy blisters have blossomed on my fingers. We are almost finished. Hot tears kiss our fingers and the dry ground. A half candle and a box of matches wait next to the shoebox. I look up. White patches begin to curdle in the black of the sky. It will be daylight soon. *We must hurry.*

# State I

I jump out of bed at four, when it is still dark, while all are still asleep in their warm lairs of turpitude and promiscuity, because the Father of the Nation, the Commander never idles around, never takes a break, never goes on holidays, never waits for the sun to shine and the grass to grow.

I am a man made of discipline. I learned it early when I was the poorest kid in my class. How they hated me. My hand-me-down clothes, my rubber shoes, my bad breath from the lack of eating, my tortured smile when I asked them for food on Christmas Eve. They smiled at me. I saw the hypocrisy hidden behind their smiles. Yes, they felt sorry for me, in their warm houses with electric light, Nessun Dorma and shit.

Yes, I grew up in filth and hatred but I did not end up in juvenile like others. I threw myself into study and worked hard, buttressed by ambition, and passed the tests to the military school with no difficulty. The army made me a man. In the army, I found light in self-sacrifice, comradeship, modesty. All my life, I have been wearing the military uniform with pride and dignity.

You do not know how much you love your country until you feel the rough fabric chafing your neck. The flag rustles in the breeze and you snap your hand in a brisk salute while standing at attention and your heart beats faster inside your chest. Only idiots salute in civilian clothes. Don't they know anything?

I, like all great men of history, am a man without a father. It was discipline, hard life, and love for my country that made me a man of power.

I am the power. I rule by heart. I give no heed to science and knowledge. I am successful because I know the soul of the people and that is not from the books, but from life. My only weapon is the heavy letter of the law, the Constitution – the word that snaps their mouths shut like the jaws of a stag beetle catching air. Nationalism is the new opiate of the masses.

I surround myself with incompetents, the ones that whisper and snigger, the ones that droop their shoulders and hang their heads in shame. I round them up like a shepherd. I do not hate my political opponents, the lettered politicians educated by Oxbridge. I really don't. I only wish they farted their guts out to curl around their necks and strangle them till their eyes bulge out like onions and their tongues loll out a foot-long like a dog's in the hot heat.

They all love me. They call me a genius. I shine like a thousand suns up in the sky. But, hey, there should only be one sun, right? Otherwise, people would be disoriented. And I care about people, Goddamnit.

When I raised to the pinnacle of power, I gave them the national self-respect. I gave them order and security. I gave them jobs. I promised them the future. I am their leader and their father. I am the president of all who wake up before dawn, of those who never take a break, of those whose hands are callused and feet are heavy, of those who wear uniforms and live from a paycheque to the next. I am the president of simple people.

When hordes of enemies came to invade our country, I turned them away from the borders. All it took was a sharp brain, one night, and a well-trained army. How they criticized me. How they adulated me. How they rallied behind me.

I sleep well at night. Yes, I do. I fold my right arm under my head as a pillow, like a soldier on the battlefield, ready to leap into action when the country needs me. Nobody knows that my agility and my stamina burst from a spartan regimen of exercise and mental training that keeps my mind and my body in the best shape. I am as brilliant as ever, inside and out.

My closest advisor, whom I trust with my life, recommended this thinking retreat. They call it a 'think tank.' It is a cube with padded walls and a simple decoration of a metallic table and a chair, both nailed to the floor. There are no windows to distract my thinking. The aides who attend to my needs are dressed in white. I quite like neatness, as everybody who knows me can attest.

I accepted to be here for my safety. There is no secret they want to kill me. That is why I never wear the same clothes again. That is why I have the shoes burned after I wear them once. That is why I have an aid taste my food. That is why nobody knows where I sleep. That is why I hired a double who looked just like me. He was subsequently poisoned, so – I guess – the rumours were true. Did they stop there? No. They keep saying that I am dying of cancer or some other mysterious disease, that I have only days to live, a few months, tops.

I am equally flattered and disappointed: don't they know I am immortal?

# An-Tan-Tiri Mogodan

You think about it over and over, rolling behind your eyes
the same pictures of that day, Friday before Easter, the *Good
Friday*, an early spring day with bees buzzing around fresh
blooms, with crisp air and sounds of dust beaten out of rugs
behind the blocks in preparation for the big day, Ermil had
just ducked out for a few hours to the lab, unable be away
from his beloved world of polymers and elastomers for too
long, back soon, he said, and the children were playing in the
front yard teeming with fragrant roses and manicured hedges
behind elaborate iron wrought fences, you could hear their
rhyme and clapping of hands, *An-tan-tiri mogodan/ Cara cara
si/ Principata mo-rin-go.*

You were busy in the kitchen, searing the chicken to make
soup and fry the meat with mashed potatoes and green salad.
The baklava you had made the day before was awaiting in the
fridge smothered in syrup. The excitement tightened your
chest and the bliss of family life spread inside you like a sweet
potion.

A black car, a Moskwitsch, perhaps, or a Lada, stopped
in front of the house and two men got out and slammed the
doors, but you paid no attention, busy with the chicken, then
somebody opened the gate, stomped on the tiled steps and

rang the bell. You rushed to the front door, still wearing the apron and drying your hands hastily on a tea towel.

Your eyes met the two men in dark suits, but your mind was numb with happiness. They did not mind and stepped inside, uninvited, scrutinizing rooms and doors and walls hung with pictures, lifting objects up in the air and assessing them with expert eyes. One man stepped into the dining room to the left and the other went up the stairs, where the bedrooms were, jumping two steps at a time and stopping from time to time to look at the carving on the banister and to touch it with his fingers.

You felt out of place and embarrassed, as you looked down at your apron and because there was smoke in the hallway, leaked from the kitchen. You were part of the house as much as the house was part of you. The rooms were high and majestic and you felt what you lacked in dignity and class was compensated by the house.

The two men said you had two hours to gather a change of clothes for each member of the family, a table, four chairs, four plates and a set of knives and forks. They said they requisitioned the house for the needs of the State. You moved around in the space around you with no purpose and a voice in your head told you it would be unwise and dangerous to oppose the decision or fight or at least react. You knew you had to do what they told you, that was the best way.

Your hands were shaking, your breath was short and your body was riddled with fear. You called the children inside and asked them to pack some things and stop asking why. You told yourself to go upstairs and pack some clothes for you and Ermil and check on the children. You climbed the stairs with the chicken in your hands and set it on the bed. The jewellery box was on the nightstand, where you left it the night before when you returned from your friends' dinner party. You opened the lid and took out the string of pearls that belonged to your mother and, before her, to your grandmother.

The rest of it blurs, except for a snippet of you with the children and some furniture and some clothes folded in a bedsheet, all crowded up together in the back of the truck, the removalists, honest people, had chucked more items in the truck than it was allowed, then Ermil appeared, surprised, smaller than you remembered, face white as paper, unable to comprehend, immobile, unable to fix it, flailing his arms and bursting into tears.

The truck drove for a while and then you recognised the Armenian Street in the old neighbourhood where merchants from Lipsca once lived after the First World War and before the second, when the city had a reputation of the *little Paris of Eastern Europe*. The merchants are long gone now and houses are beyond repair with fallen walls and caved in roofs but they provide shelter to gypsy squatters who live in squalor, ten to twenty people in one room, with no running water and, instead of a toilet, a hole in the floor.

They put you in a room in the basement of one of those houses that serves as a kitchen because of the cast iron stove against a peeled wall, a sink and the shelves askew filled with mismatched dishes, a formica table and some chairs, all covered in grime, old things picked up here and there. It is also a bedroom as there are hard beds hidden behind curtains, oily from too many hands and time, with lumpy mattresses covered with threadbare blankets. You feel the vomit when it reaches your mouth and you try to stop it and swallow it back. The stink of the basement is beyond your ability to handle it.

You are to share the fate and the room with two families, a scrawny couple and their four children, all under five, who run around and shriek all day, barefoot and covered in clothes too short to cover their swollen bellies, and an older woman whose TB keeps her in bed under a patched quilt most of the time and her husband, morose or drunk, with only a few wisps of grey hair above his ears and a round belly under a taut singlet, who often whacks a heavy hand across her face when she dares to whisper for some water.

You cry. Days pass, one after another. You face your inability to understand that you lost everything. Nothing before has prepared you for this type of life.

Your husband disappeared inside himself. You see him unable to cope, moving around aimlessly or not moving at all for hours and sometimes days, absent-minded, impervious to the outside world but dying inside, gaunt, eyes sunken in the deep of his head.

Your children cry. They are sick and coughing, sleepy, dirty, poorly dressed, hungry. They keep asking, when are we going home, and you say, we are not going home, we lost our house, there is no point in telling them lies, and they keep saying, why did they take our house, it is ours, grandpa built it for us to be happy, because he loved us, it is ours from grandpa, and you say nothing because it pains you to say, somebody else lives there now, and grandma and grandpa lost everything to the expropriation, and they were put in jail and they died there, after a while.

They sent Ermil home from the university for good, you always said his job was his life, and now his job has ended, somebody else, higher up, published his research work for a Doctor Honoris Causa title, *sic transit gloria mundi*, and Ermil sat on the bed staring at the wall where the rendering has fallen off and the bricks are eaten by water, mould and mildew, and his face held the same sadness.

They kept him in the hospital for a short while, no need to have him here, they said, there is nothing we can do, he will die anyway. You begged for a few more days, at least until he dies, you implored the nurse and thrust your last money in her pocket, it was better in the hospital than in the basement, he could have some soup and they would wash the body after he died. The next day you visited a pale stranger lying in an iron bed pushed to a paint-chipped wall with a stark light on his face from the dirty window above the bed. You had fallen in love with this man once, many years before, and you spent your honeymoon in Paris, drunk with happiness and possibilities and ignorant of the new order being installed at home.

They allowed you to take the body to his parents at Alba, a tiny village, white from the birch trees and the whitewashed walls strewn on hills, remnants of a long-forgotten convent, and you absently witnessed the funeral, with the open casket on a table in the middle of lit candles like a Homa ritual, in the old house not taller than a hut, drown in mud and poverty, Ermil's parents, defeated and dried out of tears and hope, unable to get a grip, then the mourners, old women dressed in black, toothless mounts full of incantations, crying and bending over the casket to toss holy water and wheat, place coins on the dead's eyes, then the oxcart that pulled the coffin slowly on the way of no return, and after it the cross bearers and the funeral flags, alleluia and the divine liturgy in the wooden church, and when you all went outside to the graveyard, big snowflakes, God's tears, descended from the sky on the coffin, on your heads and turned up faces, it was May, people crossed themselves, have mercy upon him and us, hands shaking with fear and belief, he was too young, the dawns too hasty.

They had *makaria*, after the burial, the sharing of food, koliva and *cozonac*, the plaited sweet bread, with thimbles of palinka. You watched them absently, then walked with the children to the river, silent and bent under undeserved burdens. Proud poplars and silver birches were growing closer to the sky and black swallows were darting through the spring air. You sat on the wet grass and held the children close, and you dropped hot tears on their heads but they never looked up but gently squeezed your hands, and the ball of pain, larger than the sky, burned inside your chest.

What happened is not a passing aberration but the reality of your life from now on.

At night, sleep eludes you and you lie in bed with your eyes wide open to the dirty ceiling. The children sleep closely nested to your body, you feel their breaths, but you are alone because a human being is always alone in the face of life and death which, to you, now, seems to be the same. You look about you, your home is a hovel with damp walls stained by smoke, with dirty cement floors smelling of urine, with a plague of fungus in the corners, with grey clothes strung above the stove, with stacks of sticky pans burned at the bottom dumped on crooked shelves. The windows have plastic sheets taped over but they do nothing to stop the draught. The cold is in your bones. You hear rodents scurry on the floor, under the bed. You snug the children closer, you would protect them from anything.

If something happens to you, if you die, your children will end up in an orphanage, those orphanages.

You sold the furniture and the clothes you brought from your house to buy bread. You have to learn that you are alone for ever. The children go to a local school every day. They get breakfast there and lunch, during the week, but you struggle to cover Sundays. They sleep better now, as they are more used to the basement, but the bed is hard and there is draft from underneath. You are worried. Anica is skinny and has not grown much but Adrian seems longer.

Your eyes get tired and watery and you lose the feeling in your hands, then the whole body gets numb. The old woman slides down from her bed and thumps on the floor like a sack of potatoes. She rocks her body from side to side. Her eyes are closed and her mouth mumbles. Her hair has escaped the woollen cap and sprawls limply on the crest of her shoulders. Her nightgown, yellowed at armpits, shows her legs of pale loose skin, purple veins and bones askew. Her husband snores loudly on his back with one leg popped out of the dirty quilt. This is your life now.

You leave the children at school and walk the streets aimlessly. You work on containing your hunger every day.

This is a big city of aligned grey blocks but this pocket of old houses must have been left over from before. The streets are empty. It feels like a small town. The cracks in the asphalt are lace on a dress from a century-long passed. Time seems to have stopped in this tiny world.

The houses look similar behind their white stucco façades, as a family. The autumn melts the trees into yellow and gold. A soft breeze takes the leaves to a waltz around the linden trees, swinging by the windows and walls. Rock doves in shiny silver plumage with green coo on cornices. Honey rays cling to walls and branches.

The air, slow and sweet, grazes at your face. Your body gets warmer in the old coat. You walk slowly. It feels almost normal, like before, except for the hunger and the holes in your stockings inside your shoes. At the end of the street, you see a small church. You glace around with caution and walk towards its door.

You step in and you drown in the silence inside, so clear and profound that you feel it on your skin. A few women dressed in black pray kneeled at the icons. Their whispers linger on the body of Christ. Inside the altar, a priest murmurs a prayer.

Your steps are timid. You look about you, then shyly cross yourself. You are not supposed to be here. But you are already at the bottom.

You exchange a few coins for three candles and move to the two trays. You light the first for your children and your heart tightens up in your chest. A second for the dead: Ermil and your parents. They were important to you, they shaped your life and now you lost them. You are alone. Tears roll down your face and you let them. The third candle is still in your hands. Your hands tremble and the thin candle snaps. The wax crumbles and sticks to your skin. You light the third candle, for yourself, and stick it in the second tray. You lean it straight against the rim.

It is so much light outside, like a gush in the sky, that it hurts your eyes. You sit yourself on a bench in the threadbare shade of a walnut tree.

"Miss Elena," a voice says, "how are you?"

You shade your eyes with your hand and you see a young woman in a faded raincoat. She bents her head respectfully and smiles, her hands together in a white union.

"My name is Neli. I am from your husband's village," she says. "From Alba. I was at the funeral."

You struggle to react and say, "Nice to meet you, Neli. Do you want to sit with me?"

"Of course. Thank you." She sets her handbag on the bench. Then she opens it and takes out a small plastic bag.

"Would you like some plums, Miss Elena? I brought them yesterday from Alba. I 've got more and I'll make some jam if I can find some sugar."

The plums are blue and longish, downy with autumn silver, and Neli opens one up in two and eats each half separately. You do the same and the sweetness on your tongue brings back times when you had fruit trees at the mansion, and a pony, and a governess, and the rich autumns that flooded the kitchen with plums and berries and grapes and apples and the women of the house fretted around big copper pots seething liquids of ruby and gold and amber.

Neli's hand lightly touches your shoulder because you are crying. She is silent for a while, then she circles your shoulders with her right arm, trying to comfort you the best she knows. It feels good to feel another heartbeat so close, now when you are devoid of affection like an empty jar waiting for the jam, when your own hands and mouth have amnesia and they forgot the language of love and tenderness, of being good and human.

"Tomorrow is Sunday," Neli says after a while when you are only sobbing, "I will come to take you and the children out. Would you like that? I live in a hostel on the campus, it is quite modest, but my three roommates are gone to their families in the country and I have the room to myself, just for us, if you want to come. I'll talk to the manager to let you in."

You smile and wipe your tears. "Are you a student, Neli?" you ask.

"I am a nurse," she says. "I work at the hospital." Then quickly, "I have to go. I am late for my shift." She gives you a quick hug and she is gone.

You are confused. You doubt yourself and everybody else. You lost your ability to trust. But you have nothing left to lose.

Only the children. Without them, there would be no fight, no struggle, just drift. If something happens to you, if you die, your children will end up in an orphanage, those orphanages. You are alone. You might, as well, be in the middle of an ocean, left alone with your thoughts, your doubts and your fears. You are sat on the bench with the new development and a small bag of plums in your lap.

Neli's room is a small box with four beds bunked in pairs and four narrow doors in the wall, the wardrobes. Four chairs surround a small table. A frayed blanket covers each bed, underneath, the shape of a pillow. Your heart warms up, you think it is wonderful here because it is clean and there are no rats. The sun has let its fingers play with the tree in front of the window and the room sparkles like a merry-go-round.

Neli makes ersatz coffee on an improvised cooker, an electric fuse inserted into a brick, and boils two eggs for the children. She has managed to find sugar and is planning to make jam in a small pot borrowed from next door. Her eyes glimmer.

You fill the tiny room with talks about better times, laughs and shrieks and the sweet smell of jam. Anica and Adrian have opened up and relaxed; rosy happiness blossomed in their cheeks. They sing their favourite rhyme and clap their hands: *An-tan-tiri mogodan/ Cara cara si/ Principata mo-rin-go.* Their words and their clapping reverberate inside you, in your head, behind your eyes, and you spin and spin, and you are in another time and another world far away, then back here in a small room filled with sunshine.

You know this rhyme they sing; you sang it as a child, too. It is a countdown for hide-and-seek but, because it is only the two of them, Anica and Adrian sing the words for fun and clap their hands against each other, left palm up, right palm down, then switch, left palm down, right palm up, then both hands up and push, then again.

"Neli, how did you manage to get a bed here," you ask, "if you are not a student?"

"I arranged it with the campus manager."

"How?" You are quite naïve.

"I gave him a lamb for Easter. From Alba."

"Alive?" The children look at her to see maybe she still has it.

"No. In a bag. One sheep had twins but we declared one lamb only." She lowers her voice, "my father cut its throat and skinned it and my mother took the guts out and cleaned it up, ready to go into the oven." She laughs. She has a twinkle in her eyes. She is younger than you, but she knows how to land on her feet.

You, who grew up without worry, do not know the fight to survive.

When the time comes to leave, your heart that has arranged itself in one of the bunk beds breaks into small little pieces and one of them hides and stays behind in Neli's little room. Anica cries a little, but Adrian, older and wiser, understands you must return to the basement. Neli hugs the children and gives them each a pair of knitted woollen socks she got from a patient.

"I will try to find you some work," she whispers in your ear when she gives you a last hug. You look into her eyes and there is nothing hidden. Not even tears.

You meet Neli in the park at the Polytechnic Institute, across the bridge from Neli's hostel. Winter is fully installed, the days are freezing and the nights are worse, the basement is a catacomb. You dread every day. You search for warm places during the day when the children are in school: the metro stations, lobbies of official buildings or some shops. You wear your coat, decent albeit thin, and you've still got your teeth.

The sun brings the shimmer of snow in your face. You sit on a frozen bench and gather the coat around you, the best you can. Neli wears a padded coat from the hospital, a *fufaika*. She is lucky. She begins talking about Ahmed, a businessman from Syria. He came here to study medicine. He owns a boutique on the campus where he sells juice and ice cream, mostly in the summer. He is well connected.

"Why are you telling me this, Neli?" You are confused.

"He needs somebody to clean his apartment: he is quite a pig," she says. "Do you think you can do it, Miss Elena?"

She took you by surprise. You try to think.

"It is not much," she says, "but it is a job. You'll get some money. He will pay after your first week, he said, if he is happy. Didn't say how much. I think you should try."

If something happens to you, if you die, your children will end up in an orphanage, those orphanages.

You know you are desperate.

"Yes, I will try." You shiver. "Thank you, Neli. And call me Elena. Please."

With every passing day, you get better and better at cleaning Ahmed's apartment. Neli smuggled rubber gloves and a face mask from the hospital for you and they make your job easier.

You step into a grey coat to cover your worn-out clothes, your own smell and your own personality. You clean the surfaces. You strip the bed and shove the sheets into the machine.

You ignore the stains, the brine of sex and the blood. You pick up from the floor soiled underwear, clipped toenails, Toblerone wrappers and used condoms. You set clean sheets on the bed and plump the pillows. You dust the credenza and the photos of Ahmed's two sets of wives and children. You clean his life in Syria. You vacuum the floor. You tidy the curtains and the drapes.

You work with the dedication of a machine, without thoughts and feelings, as if you were cleansing the world. Your hands move nimbly, going through the motions, but your mind is numb. Anaesthetised.

You spray disinfectant on the bathroom sink, the tub and the toilet, then you wipe them clean. You wash stains off the mirror and taps. You kick the pile of soiled towels dumped on the floor to the machine and you shove them in. You arrange clean ones on the rods in patterns by colour. You mop the tiles.

You remove vestiges of paid love; you stifle the place with disinfectant and you ready the scene for the next girl or, even better, if one of Ahmed's wives showed up unexpectedly, she would suspect nothing.

To clean the kitchen is hard. The food makes you vomit because you are hungry. It would be so much better if you could eat their leftovers. Less complicated. Your stomach has chosen to close itself in. You already have the bad breath of the homeless. Sometimes, Anica and Adrian save a bread roll from school and the three of you sit on a bench and share a bread roll. That, you can eat.

A half-eaten kebab lies on the table and the paper from a second one. You drop them in the garbage. You wipe the table clean and the kitchen sink. You dump the cigarette butts in the bin. You wash the ashtray and the dishes piled in the sink. You vacuum the floor. You push the start button on the machine.

You go to the balcony. The balcony is a box made of concrete and glass. When it is sunny, it warms up like a greenhouse. You fold the washing from the day before. You crouch on a low chair and cry. For one hour and twenty-one minutes until the cycle is finished. You bring today's washing and hang it on the wires.

Every day, for three hours, you live in Ahmed's apartment, you occupy a space that is not yours but you feel like an oyster inside its shell.

Every day, you clean the surfaces in Ahmed's apartment. He likes things done for him. It gives him power. He pays you. You clean. You do the job and get the money. You are oblivious to what happens there at night. You pay no heed to morality and the stains on the sheets. Nothing to do with you.

One morning, you find a girl curled up behind the bathroom door, seriously shaken and crying. You see the red bites on her neck and the bruises. You do nothing because you are devoid of affection like an empty jar waiting for the jam, and your own hands and mouth have amnesia and they forgot the language of love and tenderness, of being good and human.

You help her up from the floor and dress in her cheap clothes. You want her out of here so you can do your job. Your ears block her sobs about not getting the money and the many mouths to feed at home and the plea for a second chance. You know now the poverty and how it feels when hope is dead. You clean the surfaces. Ahmed pays you and with the money you managed to buy winter boots for both children. You plan to buy them warm coats and gloves next.

Some Sundays, when her girls are away, you walk to Neli's room, the three of you holding hands, with the uplifting emotion of going to a temple. You spend the day. Anica and Adrian bring their books and do their homework together with you and Neli. You ask them questions. They answer quickly; they are smart and they love to learn. You have fun.

You find it hard to shed the fear. You feel safe inside Neli's box. You think no long hand can reach you and the children, but you fear these visits are too good to last. You dread something will happen and stop them. Neli is more confident; everything can be arranged, she says. So confident that, one Sunday, she takes you all out for a walk in the park. She is not worried she could be seen with you. It has snowed overnight but it is sunny and bright and the snow sparkles in your eyes.

"I wanted to tell you something," she says. "There might be ears inside the room."

You learned to trust her. You look at her and wait, your heart small and scared.

"I pulled some strings," she says and looks around. You are worried about her. People who pull strings end up badly. Or simply disappear. God forbid.

"They opened the lists for apartments in the new development. I put your name down. I put mine, too, but I am single. Family is the cell of society, you know. I don't stand a chance." She smiles, resigned.

You watch the rhythm of your own breath increase, hot steam in the cold air.

"You know the new development with the Magistral Avenue in the middle that goes straight to the House of Sins? I mean, the Central Committee?"

You saw the constructions and the cranes scraping the sky. You nod.

"There are blocks on both sides of the avenue. The apartments are great: they have individual kitchens and bathrooms. Not communal. With running water and electricity."

You hold her still by her shoulders. You stare at her, "Neli, what are you talking about? Who will give me an apartment there? Are you sure?"

"Of course, I am not sure. But they build them for the people. We are people. You are people. You even have priority because of the children." She still looks in your face, confidently.

"They'll never give me an apartment," you drop your hands along your body, resigned. "My father was a boyar."

"I hear that an audience with somebody important might help."

"An audience? With whom?" You are shaking. "I can't possibly. It is too hard. Look at me. I can't be face-to-face with somebody. I will faint. Think about it. They stole everything from me and my family. How can I face one of them? I cannot pretend. I might say something. I'll end up in jail and my children in an orphanage." Your lips tremble and your teeth clatter.

"Stop. It's okay." She holds your hands, then hugs you to make you calm down. There might be eyes watching. "You don't have to do it if you don't want to. Your names are on the list, no matter what. Maybe they won't reject you. And, if they do, you have nothing to lose." She tries to encourage you.

An apartment, you think, would be great. A stable place to live. Alone, without other families. Just you and the children. And Neli, when she comes to visit. Maybe with her husband and her children when she has them.

A place, no matter how small, you will keep it clean, so clean. And warm. With a stove and a bathroom. What a dream.

"I'll do it." There is grit in your voice and a glimpse of hope in your eyes. Neli smiles.

"Are you sure?" she asks.

"I am. Who is it with?"

"Have you heard of the Plenipotentiary?" You say nothing. "He is big." You have no idea. "He is powerful. I can't promise anything for sure, but I will try to find out more."

You take a few steps in silence. Anica and Adrian are running through the snow, then they stop to make a hasty ball and throw it at each other. They laugh and blow hot air in the freezing air and strike you with their innocence.

"And this audience," you say calmly, "what do I have to do?"

"Look, I don't know much. I hear he is civilised. He is one of those new types of leaders, more modern. For the people. I don't know. Don't be scared."

You are. Neli is, too, but she knows the difference between scary and necessary.

One night, towards the end of February, when the winter is about to go but not yet, Neli comes to the basement. You are bunched in bed with the children under the quilt topped with your coat. There is a timid fire struggling in the stove, but it is too far from your bed, and it belches out more smoke than heat.

You go outside to talk with Neli. The old man is half sprawled on his bed and half leant against the damp wall. He sees you with Neli and rubs his two index fingers together on the long, that gesture that implies something sleazy between you two. You ignore him but Neli stops forcefully and strides to his bed.

"Listen, sleaze ball, if you do that again or upset Elena and the children, I'll cut your balls off and string them around your neck, like a necklace. *Capisci?*" She punches his gut with her fist. His eyes widen but he says nothing. Neli stomps away, full of courage. Outside, her knees buckle and she almost falls on the stairs. She gasps the cold air and gets better.

"The audience is next week, Tuesday." She says it all in one go, then breaths again. Now your knees buckle.

"I couldn't find out anything, though. There is a silence around this man. You will have to do your best. But be aware that he might know a whole deal about you; they say he has a good network of informers, so don't try to lie or hide anything because you can get in trouble."

"I am in trouble, anyway."

"Don't talk like that, you'll never know." You always hear this expression, *you'll never know*. It can mean many things, good and bad. She is supportive but not confident. How can she be? Nobody is these days.

"Don't say anything about the regime. Not a word. Or about your house. Show him you've changed. With the times. Okay? And I'll bring you my black suit. It's a knock-out, you know it. Do you still have the pearls? And some make-up?" You nod.

"That's it then. Good luck." And she vanishes into the cold night.

It is almost spring. The days are deceivingly warm in the morning, then you are drenched in cold rain or drifts of snow. Nothing is what it looks like.

It is the day of the audience. The cold serpent of fear glides around your neck and slithers down your back, cold and damp.

There is nobody around and you heat a pail of water on the stove. You wash and dress in Neli's black suit and it fits you well, although the skirt spins around you a little, Neli has better hips.

You passed by the building where the Plenipotentiary has his office many times, but you always thought it the House of Pensions. It lies on the corner of Regent Street and Victory Boulevard and it was nationalised in the first round of expropriations in 1950. It has arched windows edged with frosty decorations and the façade is the colour of carrot cake. It buttresses comfortably on the corner and it has only a ground floor and a first floor with balconies of white pillars, like dwarfs in the summer garden.

You change your galoshes and woollen socks to high-heeled black shoes. You hide the galoshes behind a fence and hope they will still be there when you return. If you return.

The guard, an old man with dandruff on his shoulders, instructs you to the first floor. You are expected. You knock and wait for an answer. You wait for minutes, motionless, not daring to touch the handle. A bold man in a faded suit passes.

"Please, go in," he says not looking at you.

Your hand is colder than the handle and weaker. The door swings silently and you step in. The office is spacious with a high ceiling, breathing sheer order and class. Wood panels cover the walls almost entirely. There is a thick rug on the wooden floor. A cherry wood desk reigns in the middle of the room, behind it a large leather chair facing the door. Two armchairs in front of the desk. Against the right wall, an oxblood leather sofa is ensconced behind a glass-topped coffee table. The room bathes in a warm light from the white curtain tinged with cream that covers both windows and the balcony door in the middle. The balcony door is open; it connects the office with the outside world.

There is nobody in the office. You are worried. Maybe you are in the wrong place. Twenty minutes pass and nobody comes in. You sit down after a while in an armchair, diligently, with your back straight and your hands joined in your lap. Then you stand up and step towards the door to check with the guard downstairs, maybe you went to the wrong office.

It is now that the door opens and you almost bump into a tall man, dressed in a black suit.

"Good afternoon," he says and looks at you intensely. He takes your right hand and kisses it. "Please, take a seat."

You sit robotically in the same chair where you sat before and resume your position with straight back and hands folded in your lap. He goes around the desk and sits in the leather chair. He crosses his hands on the top of a leather folder, used perhaps for official correspondence.

"I let you wait for a while on purpose," he says. "I wanted you to get used to your surroundings, to this office. After all, this office is yours as much as it is mine."

You notice the warmth in his voice, the low pleasant tone of it, somehow soothing and familiar, yet firm and commanding. He utters every syllable with dignity and confidence, somehow gracefully. His sentences run smoothly one after another, fluently, in a logical chain. Which makes you angry inside, because you cannot possibly think anything nice about this man. You hate this man and what he represents. You struggle to suppress the panic that might show in your eyes.

"I would like you to relax," he says. "There is no need to be afraid. We are civilised people. We can have an intellectual conversation." His voice does something to your inside.

The light from the windows pours on your face and he stares at you, unrestrained. His gaze touches the fine wrinkles beginning to fan at the corner of your eyes, your dry skin, the cheap lipstick uneven on your lips, your hair, dry and neglected, and the clumsy hairdo, your hands, fingers knitted in your lap, dry and roughened by detergents, the sheen in Neli's black suit from too much wear and the string of pearls in contrast with everything else.

His stare pushes you to the edge. Your nerves flinch underneath your skin. You take a deep breath. Your mind searches for comfort, for a buffer, for something to protect you from him. There is nothing.

You watch him. He is tall and wiry. His hair is straight and it parts in the middle. His mouth ends in a line on each side, like two parentheses. He looks well-fed and is clean-shaven. He has long bony fingers like a piano player. When he speaks, a spit bubble forms on his lower lip. It stays there for all the time he speaks.

"I am very happy to meet you. I wanted very much to meet you. To thank you," he says after the silence. "For the house. For looking after it so well. It is a great house, well-built and sturdy. It is warm in the winter and cool in the summer. A real pleasure to live in such a wonderful place. We enjoy it very much." He is polite and affable.

You are confused. Your eyes show it.

"My family and I live in your house," he explains. "On Lisbon Street."

The room darkens. You spin. There is a ringing in your ears. You collapse over the back of your chair. When you open your eyes again, you know you have fainted. You are lying on the sofa. He has removed your jacket and your shoes. The holes in your stockings are showing and you blush. You try to hide your feet under you.

"I am glad you are okay." He seems worried. "I asked for coffee and food. Please drink some water, you'll feel better."

You hate him. You obey and drink the water he is giving you. You do feel better. You stand up and put your shoes back on. You feel more dignified.

A waiter comes in pushing a trolley. He sets cups and a coffee pot on the glass table. Then sugar cubes, platters of cheese, antipasto and fruit, salads and eggs and a cake tower brimming with mini muffins, macaroons and cupcakes. The coffee table is laden with wonderful food you have not seen, let alone eaten, in a long time.

"Please, help yourself," he says. "This is my way to apologise for making you faint before. I am really sorry." He seems sincere.

Your hunger is bigger than you. But you fight. You cannot let him win. You cannot give him satisfaction. But you are weak. Maybe, just a bite. A small cake, or a piece of fruit, or an egg, or a sip of coffee.

He smiles. He goes around his desk and pours whiskey in two large glasses. He sips from one and gives you the other. This is good whiskey. Imported. It burns down your throat and spreads throughout your body. Everywhere. You become soft.

He says words you do not understand. He asks questions and you leave them unanswered, so he assumes and takes liberties. Your mind runs wildly, young deer chased by the lights in the thick of the night, but your body is limp. Some time passes. Outside the day grows older.

He is next to you on the sofa, your vision melts, the room folds and the wood panels bleed into the curtains, a tiny light glows on the desk but it seems far away, you feel the long bony fingers like a piano player's on your blouse, and you do what he tells you, good food makes people docile, and you turn when he asks you, and Neli's skirt is loose and easy to pull up, Neli has better hips, and his big hands are on yours, and the air of the room gathers around your skin, and your face pushes into the oxblood leather, again and again, there is a rhythm, but not because you want to, and it goes on for a while, you cannot possibly know for how long, then there is a groan, a shudder and the rhythm stops, and you hear the zipper and the door, then silence and shame thick in the room, so thick you can cut it with the cheese knife abandoned on the platter on the coffee table.

Only now you notice a door he has left open, you stumble towards it and there is a bathroom. You throw yourself onto the toilet and there it is, the cheese, the fruit, the cakes, all of it, even the whiskey and the sip of coffee, all mashed up in an acidic mess. The shame stays inside.

You fix the hair the best you can, you dab the tears and wipe the smudged mascara. You swab down your thighs with toilet paper. The stockings are full of holes, but you keep them on. Neli's skirt is intact, not ripped or anything, only wrinkled. You check your face in the mirror, but all you can see is smudged mascara and shame.

When you return, the office is empty and the food is gone. Somebody has wiped the coffee table clean and the smudge of foundation you left on the oxblood leather. The yellow light on the desk seems blind. Outside darkness pounds down on streets and houses and people. It must be five-thirty, almost six. You hear a few dull noises from the street, faraway voices and a few cars. You grab your purse, your jacket and your coat and dart to the door.

You breathe in the evening air, full of dust and smoke from old exhaust pipes. From the sidewalk, the House of Pensions seems hollow, you can see the sky through its windows. A siren wails, only a few streets away, you hear and you do not hear it. Your head spins.

You walk close to the walls, your shoulders almost touching the grey cement. You remember the galoshes and you find them behind the fence. You reach a grubby park and you lay yourself on a bench. You lift your feet up and align the whole length of you with the hard wood of the bench and put your handbag under your head. You pull your coat tight around your body and curl up the best you can. You clench the galoshes close to your chest.

You lie on the bench for you-don't-know how long, falling deeper and deeper into a void, expecting to hit rocks and drown in still waters, time fading and worlds disappearing. From time to time, deep sighs with sobs remind you of what happened.

You must go back to your life. To your children. If something happens to you, if you die, your children will end up in an orphanage, those orphanages. You must put on the old costume, the one kept in the box of shame, now idle for a while, the one that makes you vomit when you touch it, yes, that one; this costume is the life you cannot escape, and you put it on again and make it fit.

It is summer now and life is cheaper. You finish cleaning at Ahmed's and meet the children. Ahmed has paid you today and you bought kebabs and Pepsi Cola from his friends. You go to your usual park and have a feast on a bench. All three of you, happy and unhappy in your own way. Neli is working the second shift today, but she will visit Sunday.

Anica tells you the story of the man who lost his donkey. "He looked for it all over the city but couldn't find it anywhere," she says, arms large in the air. "Exhausted, he went to a park and crawled under a bench to sleep for the night." Arms crossed, resigned. "A boy and a girl come and sit on the bench. The boy says to the girl: you are so beautiful, in your eyes, I can see the whole of Paris." Pause, for effect. "And the man says from under the bench, can you see my donkey?" You all laugh, ha ha, this is so funny.

When you arrive at the basement, a lot of your neighbours are sitting on low chairs and on the ground in the dust. They stay out long into the night; they talk and laugh and the children play.

A man in a dark suit is sitting on a pile of debris. A gypsy house has collapsed a few days before. He stands up when he sees you. He hands you a letter and you sign an acknowledgement form. You open the envelope with shaking fingers while Anica and Adrian wait staring at you with wide eyes, maybe a bit worried.

You read the letter but the black signs on the paper start dancing in your eyes. You become pale and cold sweat gathers on your forehead. You are shaking.

"What is it, Mommy?" Adrian asks and there is worry on his small face. Anica is ready to cry, her lower lip quivering.

You squat and embrace their tiny straight bodies, their faces burrowed in your neck. You taste your salty tears on your lips. "They gave us an apartment." You hear your own voice, low and rusty, coming from a place where all the sorrow and the pain and the shame have settled themselves in hard slabs. "We will have our own place again. Just for us." You try to show happiness to encourage your children, to show them you have done this for them, no matter how hard it was for you. You smile and even try to laugh. The children laugh and kiss your face, wet with tears. "Let's go tell Neli."

The national celebration of the 23rd of August is two days away. There is festive vibe and red flags in the air. The ribbon-cut ceremony to inaugurate the new development is in full swing. There are apartment buildings, shops, a kindergarten, a school, a playground. The streets are straight and clean. There are even small trees planted along the sidewalks.

The Plenipotentiary gives a speech about the progress of civilisation and an unprecedented future. You listen and clap your hands, like all the people around you. You feel engulfed in compulsory happiness. Your face is set up in solemn lines and you force yourself to smile, when appropriate. Anica and Adrian, dressed in their blue uniforms with red scarves around their necks, are quiet and polite, well-behaved, as the society expects them to be.

Your eyes slide from the Plenipotentiary's face to the stage backdrop that depicts two men and a woman between them, glorifying the joy of hard work. They are bigger than real people against a blue and yellow background with red towards the horizon. Their faces are rosy with high cheekbones and square jaws. They smile widely showing white teeth. They hold tools in their strong arms and their attitude is impetuous, standing tall against the blue sky and looking into the future with confidence.

There is patriotic song and clapping of hands. Then you wait in a line to sign the papers. You write your name quickly, without reading the text, in broken lines, with no adornments, family name first, just like everybody else. The functionary shakes your hand.

"Congratulations, the apartment is yours." He gives you a set of keys. He drops them in your palm. You look down. Two golden-looking pieces of metal hooked on a ring. You feel their cold against your skin.

"Let's go and see it," children say, trotting their feet. They walk impatiently in front of you, then come back and grab your hands to drag you. You are still afraid this could be a prank, they could change their minds and evict you again and you will end up on the streets. Such a shame, Neli is at work today.

"The lift is not working yet," a construction worker tells you in the lobby. "It will start working in a few weeks."

You climb the stairs, one floor after another, two flights of stairs each floor. Your body is weak and you pant, your legs shake and you hold the banister to catch your breath. Anica is red in the face and coughing. Adrian is panting hard. You sit down on the stairs for a while. When you all feel better, you start again.

There is dust on the stairs and dots of white paint on the windows. It smells of paint and freshly poured concrete. The door has a small '84' sign on it, above the peephole. This is it: your apartment. Your best dream. One of the hundreds similar inside the compound of dozens of buildings in the new development. All the same, made of pre-fabricated blocks, grey, uniform and dull. But this one was allocated to you.

Your hands are shaking. You turn the key in the lock. You push down the handle and the door opens. Your feet are stuck to the floor. Anica circles you and steps over the threshold and Adrian after her. He looks back at you, curiously. You, too, step over the threshold.

There is a narrow hallway, a bathroom to the left and a kitchen to the right. You go straight and you are in a large room, painted white, with a large window and a door to a balcony. There is a radiator under the window.

You go back to the kitchen. A white door in the wall opens to a pantry with shelves. There is an iron sink and a pipe for gas. The bathroom has a tub, a sink and a toilet. Above the sink, a square of mirror. You twist the tap and water bursts into the sink. You jump back.

"It's rusty from the unused pipes." You recognise the two lines on both sides of his mouth.

"Do you like it?" You feel he stares at you, demanding an answer.

"Yes, it is wonderful," you say. You look down in the sink. "Thank you."

"Nothing to thank me for." He shuts the door slowly. "You deserve it." His voice comes closer, behind you. "Like any other member of the working class." His big hands travel on your hips while slightly pushing you towards the sink. The long bony fingers like a piano player's know their way around the fabrics, then they linger on the skin. They grab and squeeze and sink into flesh, then graze and shove and slap.

You abandon your palms to the cold porcelain and shun the mirror. Torrents of water burst in your ears and blood rust bubbles in your eyes.

From the room, you hear Anica and Adrian sing their rhyme and clap their hands: *An-tan-tiri mogodan/ Cara cara si/ Principata mo-rin-go.*

# Wedding

It rains all night, drums on the roof and narrow panes. On the battered windowsills, witches dance on tiptoes under flowing skirts. They put me in the dowry room. I drown in square pillows of white lace and embroideries of red flowers and green leaves stemmed with gold. Young Mother and Father, prisoners in black and white, stare down at me from below the icon. Baskets brim with blood-red eggs. On ceramics, the young shepherd holds a flute and a brown book and talks with his favourite sheep about his dream of becoming. Empty chairs line up to a long table draped in white. I am giddy from the mothballs and from what waits ahead. My life is no longer my life and my body will belong to someone else.

They wash my body and swathe it in white with flowers, pink and blue. They strum my hair and braid it round and round with sweet orange blossoms snagged into the folds.

I sing forgiveness from my parents and gypsies play the violins. Mother cries and wrings her hands and Father sweats. They send me out into the world. Gypsies smile with golden teeth shining in the morning sun. My childhood dies in nouns and verbs and buries its tiny body in the crude light of the dawn, under the soft path to the woods. The cherry tree at my window cries white petals.

Grandma hides her tears in her black headkerchief. She kisses my forehead, you are just a child. Unmarried girls leave the house with me, while gypsies play the violins. White poplars witness. The rocks in the river keep silent. Gypsies smile with golden teeth shining in the morning sun.

Neighbours bunch at the fences, knitted brows cover empty eyes, chapped lips not trained to smile, teeth missing like pickets in the fence. She is beautiful, God help her. The road is caught in the tall grass, wet with dew. My shoes are white and new. We pass slowly, unmarried girls and I, and I memorize every stone.

Godparents wait and Bridegroom waits with them in the village centre, right beside the fountain. He is young and red in the face. My body doesn't know his. He wears a suit too big for him and a tie too close to his neck. A banknote pins his lapel on a white handkerchief under paper flowers. Godmother is wrapped in crimson. Her perm is fresh and tight. She hands me a foam of white lilies stuck in a heart of green leaves.

We trudge up to the church, waking up stones, Bride and Groom, Godmother and Godfather, carrying white candles collared with red carnations. After them, parents, brothers and sisters, people from the village dressed in their best clothes, old people and red washed-faced children. My feet cry in the new shoes and blood bubbles at the heels. The sun lets its fingers play with the crisp leaves.

The cemetery climbs on a slope to the little wooden church. White crosses gleam in the sun. The air is clean and the grass is wet. Incense burns in censers and meek flames of candles lick at the morning air. The village lies in a haze. The summer is on its last breath.

Unholy hands pull ropes to swing the church bells, dormant in their yoke. The valley wakes up to a new day. I wake up to a new life.

Time is old inside the church. Jesus is stretched on a wooden cross. The little girl in me knows the gnarled wood, the brick floors, the eaten beams innocent of nails, the cracked lace carving under the roof, round and round like a belt. She learned the long saints, humble on the walls, Michael and Gabriel, the two archangels guarding the mouth of the altar, the place where the big book reigns open on the red-clothed table and where no woman is ever allowed.

It is our little church, holy from a girl saint who showed herself to those in need of believing, built from pennies and mercy, unloved by fire and foreign sword, but loved by time and people, always.

Beeswax candles burn in the cold of the church and tears of myrrh. The priest is dipped in gold. The crown of marriage is heavy on my head. The crown of marriage is not made of gold. The blood on my heels has dried. My soul wanders at the bottom of the world. We all hold hands and circle, again and again, the sacrament table heavy with symbols of marriage and flowers.

They clasped their hands in the air, fingers knitted together, a man and a woman, a man and a woman, and they go round and round, and there is happiness painted on their faces, once upon a time, there is joy and music and tying of the knots for ever, and they go round and round, with the gypsies in the middle, heads bent over violins in the velvet nest of the neck, the accordion puffing from its fat belly, and they go round and round, a man and a woman, a man and a woman.

They laid long tables topped with white paper under the trees in the garden and long benches to sit on. Shy candles in jars float in the air. Young wood crackles under bubbling pots. The pots are filled to the brim and golden coins of grease float on the top. Meat is roasted on the spit. Thick slices of sweet bread with nuts and raisins and gilded in egg huddle on plates until their time comes to finish the party. There is wine made of grapes and strong palinka for all to drink.

They sit face to face, husband and wife. They shove greasy cabbage rolls into their mouths. Orange grease trickles down their chins. He's taken off his good jacket and dumped it under the bench. Her feet are free of shoes and her perm has slouched on her face. She has eaten the rouge. His combover is messy and his skull shines in the dim light. From time to time, he wipes the sweat off his forehead. She pads her nose and chin with a white handkerchief from her purse. They drink bottoms-up from small clay thimbles. Palinka is strong. It burns their insides. Mother and Father, busy and red in the face, carry brimful plates and bottles to the table. Gypsies play their instruments in a frenzy drenched in sweat.

They've dug a big hole in the garden and bridged it with wood planks, pine and oak they chopped down for this occasion. A round split yawns in the middle, with two steps nailed on the sides. Around it pebbles to swab the mud. No need to put walls, Mother says, it will be dark. Father disagrees but he does what Mother says. Just make sure the hole is covered up well, Mother says. They'll get drunk and plonk in the shit. No water in the river can wash off the shame.

Groom doesn't say a word. He drinks palinka and stares down in front of him. He disappears, from time to time, to urinate in the garden, where the light weakens. He comes back and drinks more palinka. Godmother's gums shine in the puny light. There is a flicker in her eyes. She teeters into the garden and her heels drown in the mud. A young man waits for her in the dark. She has a fire between her legs, people say, and only young men can quench it. When she comes back, her dress is twisted around her body. Big holes in her fishnets show black hair like dill. Godfather takes big swigs of palinka and looks away.

Mother dumps food scraps in a bucket. When it's full, she takes the bucket out in the road. A sleeping beast waits in the dark. Mother tosses the food the way she feeds the chicken. They jump. Bones crackling, skulls popping, canes crunching and sticks snapping. Lumps and broken bones in filthy beaten skin covered in scars and puss and warts, poking out ribs, dirty rags covering shame of naked bodies, limping crippled bodies caked in mud and shit, chopped up hands and fingers jerking for food and drink, toothless blackhole mouths salivating and gobbling; fingers ramming, lips smacking, throats gulping, grease dribbling down in lice-tangled beards, sticky fingers rubbed on rags, God bless you.

The light is on in the dowry room. Mother comes and nudges me, it's time. My feet carry me into the house but my soul lingers outside to smash into trees, the low eaves of the house and the walls of the stable. The bed is ready, all starched and white, with big pillows and sheets with lace. She takes away the white dress. She wipes my face with a damp cloth and my armpits and between my legs. I show her the blood on my heels. It doesn't matter, she says. She leaves. I am at the window, in the dark. Outside the guests are drunk. They dance and cheer.

The music dies. Unfinished notes hang in the heavy air. The dance breaks. Sweat on the back turns to ice. They move aside respectfully. Father bows, welcome to our humble wedding,

Comrade Petrescu. Please sit at the top of the table. We'll bring you food. He bows. Mother bows, too, and wipes her hands on the apron. No need, thank you. Petrescu has rosy cheeks and a short-trimmed moustache. His guts carry the importance of his job. He is here to congratulate the bride. Where is she? I want to see her. Mother says, please come with me. Father goes in the garden and slumps on a tree stump. He puts his head in his hands. He remembers he is exhausted. Godmother drags the Groom by the hand into the garden. They are both eaten by darkness.

I hear the knock on the hard wood. The door cracks and a scream of light sneaks in. Mother closes the door carefully. Petrescu is in the room with me. He comes to the window. My heart is a pigeon caught in a burlap sack. His nails are balls at the end of his fingers. He wears a large ring with a green stone. I want to congratulate the beautiful bride. I jump back, wedged in the corner. His eyes are hard, I won't hurt you. I bolt to the door. His hands are strong. His ring bites into my flesh. The nightgown Mother has embroidered is ripped and tossed into a corner. Moonlight outside is white. White is not even a colour. Red petals cover my right eye, round and round. The night is deep and I fall in. Rivulets of blood slither.

Petrescu pulls the sheet off the bed and opens the door. Mother is there, waiting. She looks at the sheet, good, she says. From the veranda, she shakes it in the face of the crowd. The crowd cheers. Startled birds fly away. The crowd has the right to see the proof. A woman has been unmade by a man.

The man has unbuttoned his shirt and abandoned his shoes. His face glows with sweat and his eyes are vivid. His left hand is locked behind his back and the right up in the air. His finger points to the sky and shakes in sync with the music. His wife moves heavily after him, as he leads the dance, followed by another man and his wife, then another man and his wife and so on. They hop to the music and knead the mud with their feet while panting heavily. Their cheers are about married life, long and happy. Gypsies linger in the sound of their music and grin with golden teeth. The violins, melancholic and lustre with time and use, drown their sorrow far away in the sea. Tiny hammers scurry on the shimmering strings of the cimbalom. Nimble fingers flutter on the accordion ivory. Respectable brass reverberates hot air. After a while, the leading dancer changes rhythm and juts out followed by the long line. It's an angry snake chasing its own tail. Then the running mellows and they resume the hopping in one place and kneading the mud.

The new day dawns its rotten teeth. Smashed bottles and soiled plates, scraps of roasted meat and sweet bread are stuck in the mud; chairs shattered on the stamped-down grass, discarded shoes and mussed hats and passed-out Groom smudged with vomit. Daylight shrinks the houses, peels the whitewash off the walls and pulls the grass so high to choke the fences. Potholes eat the road. A few shadows lean against the night. Soon they disappear in the fog.

The two windows melt in one. The floor swells the bed up. I don't look at the bed. The ceiling sags on my head. The curtains limp. I am crumpled at the foot of the bed. I push my knees into my mouth. I swallow the pain. My colour is blue from the nape to the heel, on the left and on the right. Red roses seethe through my right eye. My life is no longer my life and my body belongs to someone else.

I go behind the house. The cherry tree is on its knees. Its leaves are turned outside like a million ears. I give my face to the rugged bark and my hair to the green leaves. I give my heart to the swallows to fly it black rags on the wind.

# We Build the Country – the Country We Build

I wake up jolted in a corner. It's dark. Under me, it rattles and shakes. I am still too drunk to care. Everything spins and I fall asleep again.

When I wake up again I am on a train in a cattle carriage. The door is pushed open and the harsh wind whirls straws on the floor. Around me men in striped clothes sprawled on the floor. Convicts. I look down. My hands are handcuffed. I hoist myself up against the wall. My butt hurts to sit on. I have no idea where I am. I ask the closest man, skin and bones. His eyes have escaped inside his head. You are on a train to the Canal. He says that with his lips because he has no teeth. I look down at my hands. This shit is serious.

My mind travels back. I was drinking at the pub with the Priest and the Cheeky one. I had a brawl again with the fag. He can't keep his mouth shut. He said I was cute and if I wanted to take a stroll with him in the moonlight. He always says shit like that to piss me off. Then he bends his wrist in my face. When I whacked him over his stupid head, two of his teeth jumped out of his mouth right on the floor like a pair of dice. He had it coming, all right. Don't know why somebody called the coppers. I saw blue and I ran for my life, but they were goddamn quicker and they copped me. Don't remember much after the blow, but I know I have a lump in my head I cannot touch now, but it's there and now I am here. My old cheese at home would be worried shit.

It takes me a while to lift myself up and wobble to the door. I feel a puke coming. It's bloody hard to walk with your hands tied when you are still drunk. I hit the walls and they throw me back. I try again and reach the door and hook my handcuffs to the latch so I can't fall over. I retch with the wind in my face and my puke flies back in the carriage. It makes me laugh but try not to. The convicts don't seem to mind. They all look down at their hands or somewhere far away with their eyes escaped inside their heads. I belch yellow bile until I am empty and sour tears roll down my face.

On my way back to my spot I fall over a few times and crush old men. They don't say a word. They wait. Their faces are eaten by black beards with smudges of grey. The skin lolls over the holes of their mouths and their bones are sharp. I settle back in my spot and I look outside where brown fields fly by, clumps of trees with almost no leaves and for miles and miles barren land. This country is ugly, I'd say.

I start thinking again and I realise I am in deep shit. This time for real. I've heard of this Canal before. All the riffraff are sent there for re-education and the political detainees and all those who happen to have whistled in the church. They build the country a canal for agriculture and navigation and shit. It's hard work from what I gather, but honestly, I never gave a shit about it. I had my life hanging around, being at the pub every night and generally busy being cool. My old cheese always said I should do something, get a job and shit, and have a family.

She worries about me. She says there are people who watch you and you'll get in trouble but I never cared.

We travel for hours and my guts eat their insides. Outside through the door, I see above the burned grass a big blue sky and a strong smell booms into my head through my nostrils. It's better than moonshine but I am not as dizzy but pleasant enough. It's the Danube, someone says. No shit. I am gob-smacked. I never saw it before, so big, solid and blue; I would stare at it for ever. My eyes water but it's from the wind.

The train stops at a station and we are ordered to get into trucks. Soldiers with automatic guns line up to force us. This shit is more serious than I imagined. Hurry up, one soldier spits at me. I look at him to say, take it easy mate, when he whacks me with the butt of his rifle. Lucky, I duck my head in but the metal digs into my shoulder. In the truck, we crowd like animals one on the top of each other in a communal stench. The truck travels over bumpy roads and dust gets in. I can't see outside cause I face the other way and a man sits on my face. This will do my head in, I'd say, and next time when I get into a brawl it shouldn't be with a faggot.

We climb down from the truck in the middle of nowhere under a big sun with dust up to our nose. We see barracks more like public toilets stuck up to their knees in yellow dust. A stocky dark man with a key unlocks our handcuffs, all with the same key, I wish I knew that. It feels bloody good to be able to use your hands again. The little man comes again, he is the brigadier in charge of us, and he takes our brigade to our barrack.

It's dark shit inside when you come from the sun, but after a while bunk beds are stacked on the top of each other up to the ceiling and all along the length of the barrack blocking the windows and they smell of fresh timber, I guess they just made them. The others put their things on each bed, but I have nothing except the shirt on my back and the pants. These shoes were all the rage some time ago when I've got them from the packet, but now they are worn out with holes in the soles but the face is still shiny, my old cheese does that for me.

Little man brigadier calls us outside on the plateau with his big raspy voice, it is time for breakfast, he says and I can't be happier, as I haven't eaten for a while being busy with other activities. We go into the mess hall they call it, a long tent made of tarpaulin held up on thick pillars stuck in the ground. We drink black coffee that tastes like shit from tin mugs and we eat brown bread with a tiny slice of marmalade, it is not quite bad but not enough, I gulp it down in one go and my stomach is still rumbling.

Outside in the sun just in front of the barrack, a pile of empty mattresses and pillows wait for us to fill them. We find hay in a hole behind the barrack and fill them. They give us clothes, rough pants and jackets made up of sackcloth shit, chunky and rough on the skin and boots from Russian soldiers killed in the last war, three sizes bigger than my feet cause nobody gives a shit, you should be grateful the country feeds you and gives you the honour to work and re-educate yourself and put some dignity in your shitty worthless life, you piece of shit and saboteur of the regime.

Next day we wake up at freaking four in the middle of the night, I never woke up so early in my life and we are out the gates at five, after bathroom, breakfast and exercise, we fucking walk on a dusty road, dust everywhere around here, even in my soul there must be some. The air is fresh though above the dust we stir with our boots and we can see the blue face of the Danube smooth and sleepy, just before the sun goes up in the sky. Little man brigadier orders us to sing military marches, as if we were soldiers or some shit, we don't know squat about music or have any talent, and we bray like donkeys to the moon, cause if we don't, the soldiers will convince us with their rifle butts right away, we don't want that and we sing the best we can.

We board on a rusty barge basked in the water and we sit on oily floor, crowded and intimate with our own dirt and the others' all together, no discrimination, all children of the same human scum. The engine of the old towboat puffs and spits and rattles but it pushes the barge down the river and we look around, it is beautiful, isn't it, outside our filth, and the bridge, massive and wonderful, with all that concrete lace up against the blue of the sky and the huge legs deep into the water, straddling the river, magnificent shit really, we all stare at it with our mouths open.

Half an hour and we arrive at the site and shovels, pickaxes, wheelbarrows, beams piled there, we hurry to get the ones still good to handle and not broken and shonky to kill you for nothing, and my mates are dissident scientists and architects, university professors and former dignitaries who were sent to the Canal for re-education, and whose hands are not used to shovel and pickaxe, and now they are full of blisters filled with blood and puss, and little man brigadier gives us a speech about the importance of this moment and shit, and nobody gives a crap, and the sun whips us from above, and I feel sick to my stomach, nothing new, really.

We shovel sand from a pouch in the hill, and it is golden sand, dry and grainy, with sparkles, we put it through a funnel to some troughs down to the barge, to be taken away to other sites of the Canal, and we get dizzy from all the digging, and the sun on our heads, I cover with a handkerchief I had in my pocket from my old cheese at home, and we are so thirsty we can fucking die, they give us just two tiny mugs of water per day and men collapse from exhaustion and weakness and disease some brought from prisons and lack of proper food and nutrition shit, and the skin on my hands cracked and my ears swelled like mushrooms by sunset, and we drank murky water from the Danube, which is not blue as I thought, but brown and it tastes like shit, but I survive, even if I have diarrhoea and my soul is a dead bird lying in the dust of the road.

Little man brigadier slaps me in the face with his hairy little heavy hands, every time he fucking wants, he says I am too arrogant and I defy him and undermine his authority and I mock the regime, that here is all about respect and obeying orders, otherwise he can kill me any fucking time he wants, cause he is in charge, and the country doesn't need scum like me, and he hits me and I feel like fucking killing him, but I can't, and he chucks me in solitary to reflect on my inappropriate behaviour.

Back in the barrack one night after solitary, I lie in bed after blackout, and I am fucking hungry, I can't contain the howl of my guts, and it's a beautiful night, we hear concert of crickets in the grass outside the barrack and the swish of tall weeds in the breeze, and we see a young red moon looking in the silvery patches of the Danube, and life could be good if we were somewhere else, and a man taps on my shoulder and gives me a slice of bread and a mug of thick broth he smuggled from the mess hall for me when I was in solitary, and I am so fucking grateful I could kiss his hand, but he says, that's all right, we are all people, and I eat and I drift into sleep and far away in an old nuns' monastery I hear cow bells and strikes on wood and every strike spills over hills and valleys, forests and mountains, and the whole country raises through the fog and mourns for her children.

Little man brigadier dashes a bucket of cold water on me, the fucking idiot, cause I slept through the wakeup fucking call, and everybody is in the washing shed now, and it's crowded and there is no chance to get to the washing basins or the crapper, and I go outside and squat with others along the fence, when soldiers come and force us to pick it up with our hands and carry it to the latrines, and there is no time to wash, and we are shoved into the mess hall.

Another fucking day in paradise on the barge, we let our useless bodies dump on the wet floor and fall into sleep with crooked necks and twisted legs and clenched hands, and I miss the chance to see the bridge, when a gunshot wakes us up, and the soldiers shout, face down on the floor, and we obey, cause we have no will or judgment, we have legs of lead and brains of glue, we execute orders and no thoughts live in our heads, we are empty, we lie face down on the soiled deck, and they could shoot us in the back of our heads, we couldn't do a thing, cause we are led by inertia, but at least we are all together like a herd of animals.

We find out what happened on the barge, that a man from Caramurat kept in solitary for long came out no longer a man, that he kept rubbing mud and water in his mug day and night whispering words and staring his eyes, that he hurled the mug in the water and jumped after it, that a soldier shot him without warning with one bullet, that the water where he sunk rippled red circles gilded by the sun like the Holy Grail, so I've heard.

The hole we dig in the golden hill is a copper bucket shimmering with polychrome fossils of plants and snails and fish and birds in its walls, a professor told me they are called that, amazing shit I've never seen before, a huge crawling snake and gigantic plants with branches as thick as trees and snails as big as a cabbage head, and it makes me think about my life, shit as it is, and short and miserable, and my Mother at home, how worried sick she must be about me, I hope someone told her I am at the Canal to put her mind at peace a bit, I hope she is still kicking when I go back, if I make it alive.

We build scaffolds in the water to carry the wheelbarrows, heavy with sand to the barge, and we get in the freezing-shit water butt-naked early in the morning to put them in, but the wheelbarrows heavy break them and men fall in, fists clutched on handles, unable to swim, and we jump to rescue them, and the soldiers are ready to shoot us, if we don't, you pigs, they are your brothers.

Long before lunchtime, we eye the Danube for the slim blue smoke of the boat, just after it gets from under the bridge, we can't stop the stomachs rumble and the brain dizzy and un-coordinated and blurry, and we dump the tools and run down to the boat to get our daily mug of broth and slice of brown bread, not much but better than nothing, and hunger follows us like a shadow coiled around our scruffy bodies all day long and at night in bed like a possessive lover when my mind floats back to our house 0when Father was still kicking and Mother kept beds of potatoes down in the cellar and smoked pork legs hanging from the beams and golden braids of onions and wreaths of garlic and big jars of pickles and barrels of sauerkraut, now we are ashamed and angry and the courage that should live in our heads and chests is gone, and so it goes these days.

Little man brigadier can eat more if he wants to, and he does, cause one morning he is white in the face with thick sweat on his forehead, and someone says he is constipated from too much shit he ate in the mess hall, but someone else says, no he's got diarrhoea from too much shit he ate in the mess hall, fact is he has to go and there is no place for that on the barge, and someone says, you can shit in the water, and he climbs on the handrail and pulls his pants down to his knees and shits in the water, and the morning breeze sprays it on the side of the barge and in our fucking idiot faces, but the thick of it goes in the calm blue face of the Danube.

My favourite fantasy in the morning on the barge is how I would kill little man brigadier and I come up with innovative ideas every morning, believe me, another one is to admire the magnificent bridge, and the third is to watch the little island choked by willows and alders and tall weeds, where a myriad of birds and fish live freely and where the villagers keep their pigs with long steppe dog legs and black snouts and feed them every morning from buckets they send over the water in boats of old men with dark beards in soiled hats, but the pigs squeal and jump in the water when the boats get close, as hunger drives them, so no matter if you are man or pig or brigadier, we all suffer from hunger, I'd say.

This Sunday morning little man brigadier comes to our barrack in a good mood and takes us to the administration building where only soldiers and officers are allowed, and we go in a room with many showers in a row and wooden grills on the floor to step on, and we wash our filth hard with soap and warm water, and we feel we are given a new body or a copious feast and a new soul or dignity and pleasure, and I am human again and not ashamed to be naked, warm air around my skin. I go back to the barrack and put on my old shirt and pants and the leather shoes that were all the rage when I've got them from the packet, and go for a walk because today we are free to do what we want, and I go behind the kitchen barrack to find some cigarette butts, and there is this Greek guy who is a cook there, and he asks me if I want to go and see the salt mountain, I say, yes why not, we are free today.

We climb this white mountain made of some shit that this Greek guy says it's feldspar, but people call it salt, and it's easy, and I am light out of the filthy clothes, lice and bedbugs, and I laugh with this guy and we run up the mountain until we reach its top flat like a dinner plate, and we run and run and look up at the sky and stretch our arms to embrace the sky and the huge white mountain, and the windings of the great river, and we spin and spin until we get dizzy and drop on our backs and we lie there as if we were dead. I dip my face into the sky and close my eyes and I am free, nobody can take me away or take anything away from me. My palms press down the rugged salt, hot like the body of a lover and I turn my head to the Greek guy lying next to me, the curls of his hair gleam black as hot tar on the white salt, and I want to touch him but I am paralysed, I stare at his profile made of sweet lines and I ask him, what is your name, Stelios, he says, and when he opens his mouth, it's pink and smooth inside like a soft peach in the summer, fuzzy and sweet, just before it's too ripe, and his body is tanned and well-knit together, and I close my eyes again and drift in a sea I never knew before.

At night the officers have festivities outside the camp, and men bribed the soldiers and brought women in behind the barracks, they ask me if I want to have a go, but I go behind the kitchen where they've lit a fire, drink slivovitz, smoke and have a good time, because we think we are free, although we know we are not, but we can dream for one day, and Stelios is there laughing with white teeth, then he stands up and stretches his arms out like he is dancing the syrtaki but there is nobody to connect to, really, but he is happy maybe drunk and I can't take my eyes away. I am young and I step back and charge and leap over the fire, and Stelios does the same, and comes back and leaps again and again, and once he doesn't and waits in the dark to catch me after I leap, and the pink lining of his mouth tastes like a soft peach in the summer, fuzzy and sweet, just before it's too ripe. I startle and glance in a bush the flicker of a cigarette and the snap of a twig and then nothing, heavy silence, we should split, I say and I go in my barrack, and I can't sleep all night tossing and turning, aroused and terrified, what is going to happen.

It's still dark and I hear the engines struggle up the hill, I roll to the other side and the neck of a rifle pokes into my shoulder and two soldiers motion let's go, behind them two officers watching, and they put chains on my wrists and ankles, and they urge me with their rifles, the other men in the barrack watch me through the dark, outside other men in chains wait, prisoners of conscience, a whisper dares in the dark, we are shoved to clamber into trucks, hard when you are chained like that. We swallow the dust, keep silent and harden up, rifles stab our ribs, sharp slaps in the faces of those who dare speak, chained to one another, we are to remain sited on the wooden bench at all times, if we try to stand up, shot without warning.

Old trucks move slowly along roads with patches of asphalt and potholes, along the river and through fields, dry like a desert, brown and poor, a few strips of crops, yellow and dry, like after the apocalypse. Men start to fret inside the truck, a brave one tells the soldier, they have to go, they have diarrhoea and stomach aches from the quinine. There is a boom and a white rocket up in the sky and the trucks stop and the soldiers cordon the area. Men clamber down and line up to the road and lower their pants and show naked buttocks to the passengers of a train that happens to trundle by, a line of ten hundred metres of men squatted down to shit on the ground in full daylight, human misery at its best, I'd say.

We stop five times to shit until we reach a sticky tar road going down the sweet slope of a hill when I look out through the parted tarpaulin curtains in the back of the truck. A blue swaddle of silk is stretched from one end of the horizon to the other, and it is stitched up to the sky, all the same only darker. My heart swells and flutters in my chest and I can't stop tears welling my eyes and I blink them down my face, and I can't wipe them off with my hands chained behind my back, but I wouldn't anyway, but let them feel on my lips, hot and salty, just like the sea must be.

# Mademoiselle

Her dull and equal steps stirred up the ordinary time inside the corridor where the slogans *Knowledge will make you free* and *The future belongs to you* contrasted with the flaking walls and the grey light that managed through the dirty windows, because the school had lost any grandeur that it might have had when it was built and because it was late Saturday afternoon.

Mademoiselle Aimée Bouchard was a reluctant note in a magnificent symphony. She was absent-minded and afraid of silence. She pushed the door open to the teachers' lounge and she was startled to see all the teachers gathered in the big room. Antoniou presided basking in his own importance at the head of a long table topped with thick glass, behind him heavy curtains and high walls covered in mahogany panels. A peep of light from the late autumn outside gave the portrait on the wall an aura of higher authority.

"Comrade Bouchard," Antoniou said. "How very nice to see you again." An affable smile crossed his face and the shiny buttons on his jacket were working hard.

"Nice to see you, too," Mademoiselle said with a timorous smile, inhibition pulling her down like heavy weights. His breath scorched her face, as he inched closer. He raised her right hand to his mouth and gently grazed its back with his lips.

"I'll just sign off and go," Mademoiselle said and her blush dwindled to cold sweat. "I see you have a meeting."

"Actually," Antoniou said and cut the air with his pudgy hand, "I would like you to stay. We made some decisions and one of them refers to you." She wilted, yet remained upright, then swooned into a chair by the wall. She glanced around, eyelids down, white knuckles clutched on her purse and meek ankles under the chair. All teachers were present: a few sat around the long table close to Antoniou, others stood by the windows, buffered by distance.

"I won't be long," Antoniou continued, confidently holding the gaze of the teachers around the table, champions of mannerisms and automatic reciters of hollow phrases, who hung breathlessly on his every word. "Comrades, our momentous responsibility and sacred mission, I would say, is to make sure that the young generations are catechized for an outstanding future." He was in love with the sound of his own voice. He once mentioned to the teachers that he would have liked to speak Spanish, a language made for victories because he loved to swirl his tongue to say *victoria* or *nación* or *tierra natal.*

"Our enthusiasm and passion for teaching and learning are reflected in the future of these fecund minds," he continued. "They are the ones who will continue our dream. But, for that, we have to prepare them." Pause and respectful silence.

"Dear Comrades, as you know, the Principal position in this school has been vacant for some time." Antoniou's stentorian voice boomed to mark momentum. "After careful consideration, the Party decided to appoint Comrade Ivanov as Principal, due to his exemplary record and his outstanding efforts in leading young generations toward unparalleled apogees of knowledge and development." As if on a cue, they all clapped their hands. Ivanov, a man in his late fifties with a bald head, rose as if tugged by a string. His broad smile revealed yellow teeth and his face failed to show surprise. Antoniou shook his hand vigorously then clasped it with his other hand like a dome.

"The other announcement I want to make today," Antoniou continued, "is that the Party decided to offer Comrade Bouchard a permanent job." Mademoiselle's blood whooshed out and cold fingers curled around her neck.

"Comrade Bouchard has been with us for eighteen years now and we consider her behaviour and her attitude toward our country's values as satisfactory. She seems to have identified herself with the obligations and aspirations of our people." This time the applause was weaker. By the windows, a few pairs of eyes glistened. Comrade Antoniou stood up, saluted the portrait, and quit the room with a spring in his step.

The day seemed like night and she walked home as though on a bridge without a handrail. Her brittle fingers tried to hide in the broken pockets of her worn-out coat. They still remembered torture and cold was not their friend.

A whole strange world was unfurled around her and she had nothing to do with it. Her suffering was part of this unfamiliar world. The stale air tightened around her. She went past a scruffy park where leafless trees stretched their twisted branches to a hollow sky, like limbs of terminally-ill patients begging for a miraculous cure, and a black bird broke the mirror of a dirty lake. Her steps disturbed the dust and the scraps of paper that littered the broken asphalt. The crumbling blocks of apartments, grey and insalubrious, were all the same, one after another.

Cold sweat broke on her forehead and her breathing became irregular. She failed to be happy, to breathe, to look at the sky. Fear began to gnaw at the edges of her heart. She remembered the nausea, the dazed mind, the insomnia, the emptiness inside even if her heart hammered hard in her mouth. Fear was still burrowed in her thoughts, where it had been for countless years.

She started walking carefully as if learning it for the first time. There was a small market, choked between two blocks, where defeated people from the nearby villages came to sell their produce. Mademoiselle liked to go through the market every day, even if she never bought anything. Today she stepped between the two rows of cement tables and took in every person and every object as though for the last time. An old woman had arranged on her table a handful of potatoes covered in dry mud, a few crab apples and a slender braid of onions. Through the holes in her knitted jacket, her traditional clothes looked shrivelled and oppressed, older than the century. Her old face, squished by a black kerchief knotted under her chin, was a living parchment of a life that meant nothing. Aimée thought that she would kiss every wrinkle on that old face just to take away the sadness and the poverty. She would shed her worn-out shoes and wash her tired feet, feet that walked the earth with no purpose, no place to go, no better.

She had gone to the market before, with her grandma, when her little shoes crushed the leaves on the soft ground and the sun played hide-and-seek between the trees. She got lost in a fabulous land of golden apples with rattling seeds inside and juicy red tomatoes bigger than her hand and fat-cheeked peppers, glossy and lazy and naughty celery that made her hands smell funny and purple long plums, downy with dew and bunches of mums she pressed her face into until it tickled and made her sneeze and the two walnuts she hid in her pocket and touched over and over because they felt funny and the taste of honey on her tongue, sweet and sticky. They were all gone now, locked away in another time, in another world, in a better world.

Today, in this world, she had run out of strength. She trudged home and, a few steps behind, the man in a brown suit was following as usual. Her uneasiness increased as she felt his breath ice the nape of her neck. He feigned interest in a shop window. She felt strangely safe.

A megaphone on a pole crackled patriotic songs out with a resigned air. From time to time, a voice would cut in and hawk slogans of wonderful times of communal living and joyful sharing, equality and prosperity for all citizens. The day was grey and the people were grey. Scrawny bodies in worn-out clothes, livid faces furrowed by hard life.

Ivanov went to visit Antoniou in his office, right after the meeting at the school. Come to see me, Antoniou had said. You are in charge now and you need to know all about your subalterns. Comrade Bouchard, especially, you must know what you are dealing with.

The imposing yellow building on the main street was one of those things people never spoke of, although everybody knew what was inside. It was quiet inside and the guard, in his wooden cubicle, looked up then in a register and nodded. On the stairs, Ivanov met a few other people but he couldn't see who they were as everybody seemed to look down and hide their faces.

Antoniou's office was on the first floor, frugal and modest with only a few pieces of furniture. He appeared to be in a good mood. He invited Ivanov to sit and pulled out a yellow file from a drawer. His hands trembled slightly.

"Aimée Bouchard," he began and leaned back in his chair. "I have to tell you that I enjoyed this case from the beginning. It is one of those cases that show you that the system works perfectly, like a well-oiled machine." He closed his eyes and grinned.

"She came from France, madly in love with the partisans' leader; they had met previously at a youth congress there. She was noticed here right away, as she became one of them, taking part in their clandestine meetings, immersing herself in the life of the man she admired and loved." Antoniou released a sigh. "They spied on her, they followed her day and night, they cornered her, they threatened her. They brought her to a point where she was so frightened that she wanted, even hoped to be arrested," Antoniou smiled, excited. Ivanov kept quiet.

"To humiliate, intimidate and destroy, that was the plan. It was easy: they barged in at night—all good house raids take place at one am on a secret date, as you know—and took her to the station. She was wearing her nightdress." Antoniou stopped and closed his eyes.

"Soon they started the ordeal to fray her nerves: the beatings, the screaming, the foul language, the humiliation, the repeated interrogations, maybe a bit too harsh, those brutes who slapped her in the face with the back of their hairy hands. They shouted at her." He started reading from the file, with a twitch of a smile on the corner of his mouth. "Why did you come to our country? You fucking French bitch. To destroy it? To instigate? To undermine the Party's authority? Why are you against our people? Tell us your friends' names. Where do you meet? You don't remember, ha?" He looked up at Ivanov. "One of the interrogation officers, a big guy named Twinkle, he'd lost one eye in a brawl, almost illiterate but faithful to the cause, was particularly keen to get results. I'll make you remember the milk you sucked from your mother's nipples, he threatened her, you disgusting piece of French shit. And I hope you like stripes 'cause you'll be wearing them for a long time." Ivanov had stopped taking notes. He listened respectfully and played with the pen.

"They followed the procedure: the sharp jets of cold water to bruise her skin, her bones and her soul, the rats in the bed, the lock-up in dark rooms for days not being allowed to sit, the sizzling lights stabbed in her eyes. They let her starve for weeks, then they gave her food, plenty of good food, to show her she was weak and passive, nothing more than a slave of her own needs, a slug with no will and no dignity. They were right: she ate it and vomited and passed out and vomited again."

Antoniou's voice became melancholic. "They murdered her last speck of dignity when she had to relieve herself on the floor of her cell. The hot jet trickling down her legs splashing the coarse fabric of her dress and, right after that, in a convulsion, a steamy load dropped in the back. She passed out. They revived her with a bucket of cold water and she threw up a green liquid all over the cell floor. That was the cherry on the cake," Antoniou grinned and put his hands behind his head.

"Only after they turned her into a shadow, did they release her. They let her go, not in pain but in fear – fear of what could happen next, fear of the unknown. It says in the report that she kissed the ground when she stepped out of jail."

"Interesting," Ivanov said.

"She was confined to live in our town and teach French. When she arrived she understood that freedom is an illusion. Follow the rules, I said to her, do what you are supposed to and you'll be right. If you can't we will help you, but if you won't we will make you. That's how it goes."

Monday morning dawned disciplined but grim. Antoniou thought it was his turn to visit the school to see Ivanov in his new position and to check on Mademoiselle. He was quite pleased with Ivanov's performance. He had been Ivanov's mentor and was instrumental in his appointment. In the promotion report, he called Ivanov "'the firebrand who peddled the Party's most daring causes" and said that "his arms carried the revolutionary standard towards victory." In reality, he considered Ivanov no more than a dilettante, a mediocre guy who lived his life according to an ambitious plan. An apparatchik, nonetheless the Party needed people like Ivanov.

Comrade Mona, Ivanov's secretary was not at her desk. Antoniou pushed the door to Ivanov's office and almost bumped into Comrade Mona trying to get out. Her tight skirt was twisted and the skin between her breasts revealed by the plunging neckline was slightly clammy. The pink lipstick she had applied to cover a succulent cold sore was smudged and her hair mussed. She smiled broadly when Antoniou's hand, en passant, rested a few moments too long below her waist where the skirt zipped in the back. Her eyes said to him she could do unexpected things.

Ivanov was leaning back in his leather armchair, his tiny body filling it like an undernourished baby in a too-large crib. Antoniou surveyed the new Principal's office: omnipotent desk, leather chair, bookcases along the walls, big windows, heavy curtains with paludal pattern and soft rug. Outside the window, on the top of a hill, a cement factory spreading dust for miles around was the image of the future: the industrial revolution.

They shook hands and sat down. Comrade Mona brought coffee, real coffee not ersatz, perhaps from the packet.

"How are you travelling?" Antoniou asked.

"Can't complain," Ivanov answered. "A few problems, here and there. Nothing we can't manage."

"Very good. You might want to know that the 'Sofia Negus' case is now closed. You know, the girl in the tenth grade who got pregnant." Ivanov nodded. "They found a quack to do an abortion," Antoniou explained. "A former nurse, some said. Others, an illiterate woman, nothing more. The blue-eyed guys had been watching her for some time. As it happened, someone whispered and they got her. Put her away, for good." Ivanov was listening, respectfully. "But you know," Antoniou continued, "something went wrong with the girl. She got sick. Complications. She was refused medical care. An infection. Antibiotics could have fixed it. Easily. We let her die. To teach a lesson. To set up an example."

A knock at the door interrupted them. Comrade Mona came in smiling, trying to show professionalism. She had fixed her hair and her clothes. The lipstick was still messy because of the cold sore. The possibility of unexpected things was still in her eyes.

"Comrade Principal, we have a problem," she said in a rush. "Comrade Bouchard didn't show up today. Her class is alone and it's making a racket on the second floor."

"Are you sure?" Ivanov asked pretending to be worried when, in fact, he enjoyed the news. It was his first real problem to solve as Principal. And Antoniou was there to see his managerial skills at work. In his own head, he was a crisis master.

Antoniou rose from his chair.

"Maybe we should pay her a visit," he said and couldn't contain a sneer.

When they arrived, above the block, there were wisps of clouds hanging low on a jaded sky. The wind rose from under the world and blew away rubbish and dreams, spreading the grit over people's faces, forcing them to open their eyes.

Ivanov opened the heavy door and let Antoniou in first. They were greeted by a smell of boiled cabbage and urine. The lift was not working due to power cuts during daylight hours. They were not used to climbing stairs and, when they reached the top floor, they were both panting heavily and large patches of sweat darkened their shirts at their armpits and on their backs. Ivanov thumbed the doorbell while Antoniou inspected the surroundings. There was no answer. They waited for a minute or two. Still nothing. Antoniou's knuckles met the door's wood hard, twice. Silence again.

"I've got this from the Housing Department," he said and pulled a key out of his pocket. "I had it with me, just in case." He turned the key in the lock and the door opened with a squeak. They snuck in with caution, Antoniou first and Ivanov after him, a step behind, respectfully.

Antoniou was stunned. He looked around and couldn't believe it. "I'll be damned," he said. He waddled into the bedroom, awkward and too big for the place, then in the kitchen and the bathroom. He was pale, dripping with sweat. The small room was completely empty. The linoleum was still showing the prints of a bed and a table. The kitchen was incredibly narrow and, on one wall, a small suspended cabinet was also empty. The air was cold and it smelled of poverty.

Ivanov felt Antoniou's hard gaze burn on his bald head. He stared down at his shoes. His suit felt too big.

"Will you excuse me," Antoniou said and went into the bathroom. There was no door and Ivanov heard Antoniou's explosive relief splotch inside the toilet bowl and didn't know how to take the smell. He heard him pull the string to flush but there was no water due to economy cuts during daylight hours.

*She broke the time and she smells hope*
*Of freedom, and sun, and rain from the clouds*
*Advance, comrades, behold the promised land* Ivanov could hear, muffled, from the megaphone outside.

He stepped toward the window where a curtain of undefeated white waited patiently and maybe a bit shy. It was the only thing left in the apartment.

# The Little Girl Has Curly Hair

The little girl has curly hair. In the morning, the mother untangles it with a plastic comb. She pulls too hard. The curls are stubborn. The little girl cries. The mother gives up and ties it in a rubber circle so tight that the little girl can't close her eyes.

They go out in the fields. There is dew on the grass and the heat cuts the heart. The little girl doesn't like going to the fields. She wants to stay at home. To climb in her cherry tree and hide among the leaves. To love its silvery bark with her tiny fingers. Silvery and shiny like a fish. The little girl would spend the whole day buried in her cherry tree.

The mother carries food in a basket made of willow sticks. The little girl follows her with small steps. The mother also has a boy, older than the girl. The mother doesn't take the boy to the fields. The boy stays home and plays football with other boys.

The little girl follows the mother up the hill, on the narrow path at the edge of the forest. She carries her mother's hoe. The mother carries the basket and the clay flagon for water. The mother's feet clamp down the soft ground. The little girl hopscotches outside the mother's footfalls. Her prints are small and narrow like a doll's.

The potatoes grow in long lines of bushes. The little girl can't see the end of the lines. The potato flowers are white stitched with yellow. The stalks are glossy.

The little girl uproots the weeds with her tiny hands. The mother comes after with the hoe and cuts off the weed roots and breaks the dry soil. The little girl has to work fast. She is scared of her mother's hoe.

The sun climbs up in the sky. Salty sweat trickles down the little girl's face. She wipes it off with the back of her hands. The mother urges her to go faster and faster. The little girl would like to stop. Her tiny hands are full of blisters and dirt. The sap from the weeds is green with a tinge of yellow. It seeps into her broken skin and burns. The dress she wears was her mother's. The grandmother has sheared off the puffy sleeves and the chunky skirt and folded the wide split at the neck into a safety pin. It feels lighter now.

The mother sends the girl to fetch water. The clay flagon is heavy. She drags it through the high grass. The grass is a green carpet speckled with red poppies. The white patches are bindweed. The little girl squats and plucks a tiny white flower. It's a sparrow's skirt. It feels soft to her cheek.

At the edge of the grass, there are milk thistles with tufts of purple flowers. The little girl stays away from milk thistles. They are prickly and can hurt her. The little girl loves the mulleins. Tall and dusted with silver. She thinks they are the big candles she saw in the church when the grandmother took her. When she saw the baby Jesus clung to the folds of his mother's robe.

The little girl knows all the plants and flowers. She stoops down. She listens. She sees the sorrel hiding under the high grass, rusty with heat. She breaks a few leaves with her tiny fingers. She puts them in her mouth and chews. The sorrel is a bit sour and tangy. The little girl loves the sorrel.

The little girl steps into the forest. Her tiny feet know the way. The forest is full of voices and pine wind. She is not afraid. Her feet are tired. She takes off the hard shoes. She steps on a carpet of shiny needles that don't hurt her soles.

The spring whispers from the heart of the mountain. The little girl lays herself on the black-green moss. She dips her tiny feet in a nest of water. She plucks a burdock leaf from the water and rests it on her face. The burdock is bigger than the little girl's face. She closes her eyes. There are whispers. She is not afraid. The sun is playing with the leaves. Her feet are pins and needles. She doesn't move.

The mother comes pounding the ground and slaps the little girl across the face. Then she turns around and disappears. After a while, the sound of her dies. The trees are silent. The spring has stilled. The little girl fills the flagon and starts walking back. The flagon is heavy and her palms are burning.

The sky colour moves at noon. They sit under a plum tree. They have made a whole in the high grass and set up their basket. The little girl is afraid because the high grass has moved. She is afraid but she doesn't say a word. The mother peels boiled potatoes and sprinkles salt on them. She gives one to the little girl. The sun falls over the fields. The little girl eats her potato and thinks about rain. The little girl knows the clouds are pillows in the sky. She knows the rain comes from dirty pillows. She could go home if it rained. The sky is blue and clear.

The little girl pulls weeds all afternoon, chased by the mother with her hoe. Her tiny legs give up a few times. The mother waits until the little girl can stand up again.

The little girl has no memories. Green meadows behind her eyes she can run to and hide. But she likes the smell of rain. And the taste of green apples on her tongue. Because they are not ripe they taste so sour that the little girl closes her eyes when she eats them.

The mother is busy at home. She milks the cow and feeds the pig and the chickens. The little girl carries a bucket of water for the cow and another one for the pig and the chickens. The mother goes into the house. She pours the milk through a sieve blocked with gauze to keep away the dirt. Then she covers the pot and stores it in the cellar to make cheese later.

The house has only two rooms. The kitchen is the small one. The mother has lit a fire in the stove with thin sticks from the garden. The fire crackles and makes the polenta bubble in the cauldron. The mother chops tomatoes and peppers. Thin shreds of meat sizzle in hot lard. The mother adds the tomatoes and the peppers to the pan and covers it with a lid.

The boy comes into the house. The mother says, go and get your father. The boy runs out.

The father walks home, drunk from the pub. His lazy feet wake up the stones asleep on the road. The father swears at the stones. They are in the wrong place. His swearing stirs the dogs. The dogs bark and taut their chains.

The front gate opens and the father comes in. The little girl's chest is shuddered by a sigh. The sigh is too big for such a tiny chest.

The little girl goes into the garden to the cherry tree. It is almost dark. The little girl wants to live in the cherry tree instead of the house. She likes it at dusk when the house and the stable and the chicken coop, all disappear. She opens her eyes and all she can see is piles of darkness, faded and blurry.

Go and get your sister, the mother says to the boy.

They sit around the table. The mother and father shout at each other. The father is drunk. The mother is red in the face. The little girl is afraid. She keeps her chin down in her chest.

She is afraid to look up or eat. The boy is not afraid. He eats the stew with big chunks of polenta.

The father is angry. He stands and flips up the table. Plates smash and clatter to the floor. The red sauce jumps on the wall. Hot polenta sticks to the little girl's chest and neck. She is so afraid she starts crying. Her body is shaking. The father turns to the little girl, why are you crying? The little girl has frozen. He grabs her by her ear and throws her out of the house.

When night comes, the little girl is not afraid. She understands the night. Night is a good place to hide. But at night, the little girl has a nightmare. She wakes up but doesn't cry. Or move. The pallet underneath is wet.

The little girl sleeps with the mother. Tonight, her side of the bed is empty. The mother has gone to the other bed where the father sleeps. The boy sleeps alone. The little girl hears the mother in the father's bed. She doesn't understand. She doesn't want to understand. The little girl is happy she is alone in the bed.

The mother comes back from the village. She brings back a blue plastic bag. She calls the children into the house. The grandmother doesn't need to know. She has two éclairs and gives one to each child. The éclairs are topped with chocolate and filled with vanilla cream. The boy gulps down his éclair quickly. The little girl takes a tiny bite and chews it. The mother asks the girl to give some of her éclair to her brother. The little girl says, no. The boy punches the little girl in the head and snatches her éclair. The mother laughs.

The mother is away, in hospital. So they don't have another brother. Or sister. The grandmother looks after the children. The grandmother doesn't pull the little girl's hair in a ponytail. The curly hair is free. The little girl climbs into her cherry tree and the grandmother doesn't scold her. She calls her when the food is ready. The grandmother's house is only one room, with a stove and bed and a little sink. The little girl loves her grandmother's house, tiny like the seven dwarfs'.

The mother comes back from the hospital. The grandmother calls the children. The little girl hides behind the chickens' coop. The boy says to his mother, welcome home, mommy.

# *Purity*

The room has become cold overnight. She has been up for hours, maybe all night. Her back is stiff and she cannot feel her hands. Her legs ache from the cold. She moves to the window. She leans her forehead against the curtain and feels the dust in her nostrils. People go to work at this hour. Their footsteps clack on the stones. She is one of them, a worker in the curtain factory, and she would normally leave now, too, but today she has a good reason not to go. It is Saturday in the house and it is March outside in the street and still cold.

She gazes around the small room, familiar to her by now. The wallpaper is yellowed by time, peeled at the seams by water and baked by heat. The faded print of the Virgin Mary with the Child, she stared at many times trying to see a line in her face glowing with beatitude, and the floorboards buckled from moisture. An old wardrobe and a lumpy bed are all she can afford, but she has been happy here. This room is where she learned to live. The job at the curtain factory pays enough to send money to her mother and cover for this room and a meal a day. All she has left is a few coins for the bus fare. She was lucky.

She opens the door and steps quietly into the narrow hallway. The family she lodges with is still asleep. She leaves the light off in the kitchen, as she knows her way around and the street light spills in a bit. Last night she went in the street and brought water from the well, so now she just fills a large pot and starts the stove to heat it for washing.

The kitchen is cold and she folds her arms around herself, missing somebody to hug. She sways her body from side to side. A smile flutters on her face. How well she remembers the first time she saw him, Stefan, the love of her life.

They were waiting in line, at the factory, one Saturday after work, to get their wages. She felt his gaze in the back of her head. She turned and blushed. After that, he sought her company every day. She was shy at first; her mother never let her talk to boys when she was at home. They went to the movies. They sat in the back section of the theatre and he kissed her in the dark. She was so surprised and happy she almost fainted.

She has never been kissed before and she was more aware of the warmth of his body than she was of his mouth. She would have liked him to tell her he loved her, more than anything, with all his heart and with all his being, now and forever, but his lips were hot and an inch away from her ear and she was giddy and hot inside her clothes. She wanted to offer herself to him, fully and unconditionally, and let him do with her whatever he wished.

On the way back to her house, they held hands. The streets were quiet and dark, only dull yellow lights on wooden poles, here and there, at intersections. They stopped in dark places from time to time to kiss. She turned her face up to him, as he was taller, and above his head, the sky was crisscrossed with tiny stars, timid and far away. In front of her house, they kissed for a long time, as she was not allowed to bring men in the house. He kissed her one last time, sighed and said good-night. After a few weeks, it was only natural for him to asks her to be his wife. She accepted.

A glance at the clock on the wall tells her she has enough time. She carries the pot to her room and fills the basin. She shrugs off her clothes, the faded gown that overlaps in the front, and the old pyjamas, threadbare at the bottom and on the back, and sets them neatly on the bed. It is in this bed where time became fluid, when she lied awake, night after night, dreaming. About him, about their life together as husband and wife.

She will be married – she, Lizzie, the poor girl from the country with no dowry. She will be a wife and a mother. She will be treated with respect. She will have a better life than her mother had. She sees the poor house in the village, where she grew up, cold and mouldy, with only one pane of window, where all of them lived and slept on hard beds, her mother overwhelmed and tired, pregnant most of the time she can remember, with small children clung to her skirts, and new babies born after her father passed. She knew, Lizzie, it would happen to her, too, as she was grown up now and her breasts blossomed under the dirty dress, and they, the men, began to notice; she knew she would have repeated her mother's fate, had she stayed, so she left to find work in the city.

Yes, she was scared and it was hard, especially as she is so shy and with no man to protect her, but she found this job in the factory and she keeps her head down and pretends she is a bit thick in the head, even if pretty, so the foreman and the others throw words at her nevertheless, as they do with all women, but she gives no response and keeps working. Now, she will pretend no more; she will be a married woman, with a man at her side, to love and protect her. They will have children and the factory will give them an apartment, in one of those new blocks with white walls and big windows, just off the main street.

She sinks the washcloth in the warm water and rubs the soap on it. The skin turns red under the light pressure of the washcloth, especially where she insists, under the arms, along the neck, below the hair caught up in a bun, on the breasts. She sets the basin on the floor and sinks her feet in the water. The washcloth travels along her shins and calves, her inner thighs and hips, leaving streaks of soapy sheen in its wake. Then she pours clean water with the porcelain pitcher and the water follows the lines of the flesh and makes it shimmer in the morning light.

She hugs in the old towel to dry and she feels, under the skin, a soft tremble of excitement, a glance of the happiness that awaits her. She wraps herself in the same old bathrobe and sits on the bed.

One night after work, she was moving with the crowd out of the factory, when a woman caught up with her from behind.

"He promised another girl," the woman whispered in Lizzie's ear, "in his village. He won't leave her. They have a child together."

Lizzie froze like struck by lightning. People were streaming out of the factory, around her. Some laughed at her, others pushed her, other – men – put their arm around her shoulders, "I'll take you. For a night or two." Her face was as white as milk. Nausea invaded her body. On her way home, she ran like crazy, forgetting to avoid the rain puddled in potholes, then she stopped to catch her breath, leaning against a pole. She remembered the words of an old woman in the village, when she was a child, that happiness is something you must fight for. That night, she had no supper; she dragged herself into her lumpy bed and slept until the next morning.

A crude light peeps through the window and clings to the edges of the objects. They all seem drained of life now and Lizzie hunches her shoulders under the weight of time. She dashes the tears away with her fingers and cups her face in her hands. She brings up his image behind her eyes. The way he looks at her. A smile skims her lips. His eyes, green with little yellow specks like a handful of gold sprinkled in the middle. And that sliver of hair tumbled forward along his right temple as if rebelling against the mass of his hair slicked down with oily pomade.

She opens the wardrobe. A white dress hangs solitary in the cold air. A girl at the factory has stitched it from leftover lace. Underneath the lace, a lining of white cotton gives it a look of purity.

# Rite of Passage

Every morning he rode his bicycle to university. He worked in the morgue. His job was to prepare the cadavers for dissection for the Surgery 103 – Anatomy course. All entering medical students had to take it. The cadavers came to the morgue already prepared. His job was to pull a white knit sock over their heads and hands, nothing more. For the fresh students, the first encounter with a dead body was a rite of passage, but for him, the vaguely human forms under blue bags aligned on stainless steel tables in the cold silence of the morgue were friends or acquaintances he could have met in another time.

He carried a war in his face and a dead soldier's boots on his feet. In the summer, his feet were red and itchy and they peeled skin, but the war in his face was always there. He maintained a furtive look, as if ready to cross the border illegally at any moment. His hair had deserted him early. The top of his skull was bare and he used to do the combover until somebody said, *be a man, shave it off.* So he did. He blinked hot tears down his face, in front of the mirror, not because he was sad to lose his last hair but because of the pain. The same way he sheared the terminal syllables off his name, which was once a real name, the kind you could track on a map of Eastern Europe.

They hated him at the university and called him "the creepy guy from the morgue." They played sour pranks on him and he felt miserable most of the time. Every night at home, he attempted to kill his dejection with big glasses of cheap red wine he drank while chain-smoking and dreaming about killing them all.

The war in his face was more obvious at those times.

He knew it was wrong to think that way, but he had seen worse. He was okay with death. He read thick medical books at night and he was fascinated with terminal diseases. He imagined the moment when all hope was gone and the serenity of imminent death. *This one is finito*, he said every time he read about an incurable case. Or, to another with emphysema, triple by-pass surgery and a pacemaker, *mate, you should stop smoking, you are gonna kill yourself.* From one of the thick books, he learned that his clubbed thumbs were the sign of a genetic trait called brachydactyly type D, or the "murderer's thumb," as the fortune-tellers called it.

One day at work, he was more morose than usual. They had laughed at him all day and he overheard two cleaning women mocking him. *I don't think he's got what I need*, one of them said. He knew her, she was overweight and he felt closer to her in what he thought of as freaks' solidarity. To make the day even worse, someone had stolen his bicycle and he had to walk all the way home in a heat that melted the asphalt. All he could think about was his colleagues – dead in his imagination, their bodies decomposing in the heat. He would be glad to pull the white knit sock over their heads. When he entered his house, it was dark and cool, maybe a bit mouldy. He ignored the dirty dishes in the kitchen sink and the mounds of clothes on the oppressed couch in the lounge; he discarded his boots, grabbed a beer from the fridge and went into the back garden.

The space was wild: young trees and old trees, shrubs and bushes, overgrown hedges and timid water features strangely intertwined like crippled arms of old men grappling plump breasts of young girls. Dainty flowers once emanating sibylline fragrances were now choked by prickly poisonous weeds. He loved the vegetal anarchy of his garden and he wouldn't change a thing. Only in the front yard had he planted pansies. He called them violas: purple with yellow streaks, ink blue, red speckled with pink, tender white, azure blue. He would touch the velvet of their petals and the tremolo in his fingers would cross his whole body. He would close his eyes and drops of sweat would stud his bald head.

He sat on the ground and rummaged in his head for a solution. *Go back to where you came from.* He'd heard it numerous times. He hated them, too, their easy-goingness, their down-to-earth and nothing-to-lose attitude, the laziness of their history, their sadness-free past. No deaths, no anger, no iron fingers clutching, piercing your soul. No war to carry in their faces.

There is no racism in death. Death is uniformity. He drank more beer, then wine. He smoked many cigarettes but no brilliant idea came into his head. He stumbled into the house when he could no longer see his hands and fell flat on the rumpled bed, a mess of faded sheets and quilts, of inebriated twitchings and nightmares.

In the morning, the hangover added to his normal depression. He caught the bus and got a seat. People moved away from him because of the stench. At work, he prepared the bodies for a new series of students. The scent of embalming fluid hovered in the air more intensely than usual. After class, he closed the blue bags and put the cadavers back into the cooling drawers.

The cleaning lady came to wash the floor. His blatant stare attacked her full body, while he remembered what she'd said the day before. He followed her to the back room where she went to empty the bucket. There was a wide sink against one wall and a large stainless steel table on which he prepared the bodies. She dumped the bucket and then wiped the table with a cloth. He came behind her and bumped her down onto the table. She giggled. His pants with the heavy buckle fell with a thud on the dead soldier's boots. His hands with clubbed thumbs pushed down her shoulders to squish her ample breasts against the cold of the stainless steel. It was like an order. His hands fumbled to lift her grey coat and groped for her privates. He put two fingers inside her and moved them in and out. The woman groaned. He took the fingers out of her and hooked them in her mouth. I am disgusting, he thought, but it felt good. He pushed himself inside her and started thrusting, skin hitting on skin, harder and harder. The woman's body shuddered and her mouth was crammed by his fingers. Sweat streaked his bald head and trickled down from his armpits. He remembered the green meadows of his childhood, the old photos in the good room, the geraniums in the window, his first taste of grappa and the poverty. He closed his eyes. He felt liberated. Tears welled in his eyes.

He found the bicycle in the carpark: rims bent, tyres slashed and no chain. On his way home, he carried the sun on his head and the dead bicycle on his shoulders. He went into a shop and bought bread, milk, red grapes and English breakfast tea. At home, he examined the mail and sorted it into bills to pay and others. When the heat mellowed, he watered the pansies and pulled out a few weeds.

He went into the scruffy garden and began to cut the overgrown branches. One by one, as if ordering books on a shelf, alphabetically or by genre.

Rain came down from the sky. Big heavy drops that startled the leaves. They fell on his head and he took it as a kiss. He spread his arms. He took off his shirt and twirled it above his head. He remembered a dance they had taught him in school. He kicked his heels together and stretched his arms towards imaginary dancers on both sides. He heard the music, it was all there, and he was floating with all the others. And the whole village looked on.

# But Deliver Us from Evil

That night, on the 21st of December 1989, I was late but I rushed madly to be in the apartment before six pm because every night they cut off the power at six pm. With the candle and the matches in hand, I sat at the kitchen table ready for two hours of staring into the flame and thinking about our lives. The light in the ceiling, yellow and shy, stayed on but I couldn't move, paralysed by surprise. *Maybe they are just late.* I went to the sink to get a glass of water, but my shaky hand turned the hot water tap instead of the cold. The water was hot. *We have hot water.* I put both hands under the tap and let the boiling water pour into my cupped palms until they turned red and I couldn't stand it anymore. We hadn't had hot water in many years. That's why the water was reddish, from the rusty pipes.

I dashed into the bathroom and let the hot water run into the tub. I didn't turn the light, I took off my clothes, I knew my way around the tiny apartment blindly, I sank into the water, I was used to the dark. There was so much water around me. I was skinny, we all were. I got dizzy and closed my eyes. In a long time, a warm feeling seeped through my veins. Happiness? I was scared to be happy. Fear was there, in every cell, in all of us. I remembered that on the train, coming home, people were smiling and talking to strangers. *God is on our side*, someone said.

I lay in the water until it went cold and then I dried myself still not believing that we had hot water. Loud voices in the stairwell froze me in my tracks. *Let's go. We all have to go.* Hard knocks on the doors, including mine, but I didn't move and I didn't breathe. Normally the raids were at the early hours of the morning, but now it was evening. I heard a few more noises, doors shut carefully, then quiet again. I looked through the peephole: it was dark and quiet. I put on a bathrobe and waited.

I learned the tiny apartment as though it were part of my own body. Even now, after many years, in the world behind my eyes, I can still see all the drawings made by paint patches and smoke on the walls. I knew every cut in the linoleum and every spot where the paint peeled on the window frames. Till the day I die my toes will feel the cold from the gap under the front door and the mould in the cupboard will for ever dwell in my nostrils. The toilet seat had a screw missing so I always sat on it carefully. The skin on the tips of my fingers still dreams at night about every crack in the paint of the radiator for I touched it billion times to see if it was warm (it wasn't). When hot tears I couldn't hold in welled my eyes, they clung to the bathtub rust that looked like flowers and clouds and angels.

I stood motionless, my back against the cold wall, my hearing magnified that I could hear people breathe in the other apartments. They, too, were motionless in their cold empty kitchens or huddled together in their cold empty bedrooms. A thick silence swabbed the houses and the blocks. *Something happens somewhere else.* I couldn't feel my legs. My body was alien to me. All lights were off but, in the kitchen, a friendly light was spilling through the short curtain onto the table. *The moon is on our side, too.*

I looked outside: from the fourth floor, everything seemed deserted. The small houses on the other side of the street were even smaller that night. Timid lights here and there. The road was wounded by dark potholes. The sky was close. At this time of the year, it should have been cold and snowing, Christmas was just a few days away. At the thought of it, a cold hand reached inside me and switched something off. We were not allowed, there was no food, there was no joy, there was no Christmas.

I remembered then the first Man who couldn't endure beauty: the sky in the spring was too blue for him; Eve's smile was too beautiful; even the clouds and the flowers were too pretty. Crushed, he confessed to God that so much beauty hurt his eyes and he wished to be blind. God listened and, in his infinite wisdom, gave the Man tears, many tears.

I looked at the sky again and my tears dried away. Behind the blocks and the houses, the sky was lighted. I opened the window and I heard gunshots. I hadn't heard gunshots before then, but the chill down my spine told me they were real. *People are dying out there.* I shut the window and cowered on the floor. Then I crawled to the bathroom. *I need the radio.* At eight, Radio Free Europe had a Romanian language broadcast. I scuttled into the room, grabbed the radio and went back into the bathroom. With trembling fingers, I turned it on. *The revolution has started* jumped out. The voice was excited and scared. My heart jumped into my mouth. Hard hammers drummed in my ears. My hands startled and dropped the radio. It smashed on the floor and shattered into a million pieces. I stared at it in disbelief. I had saved for months to buy it. It was my only connection with the world outside. *What am I going to do now?*

*I know. I am going to make cabbage rolls.* I thought it was a good idea. I had some mincemeat from a neighbour who had woken up in the middle of the night and waited in a line at the shop with a lot of other people, for five hours, to buy meat or whatever they brought in. She gave me some, not much. My mother from her village sent me cabbage pickled in brine and a few eggs, so I had everything I needed. I was lucky.

I went into the kitchen, put a blanket over the window and lit the candle. *Our Father which art in heaven, Hallowed be thy name.* I took the cabbage leaves one by one and carefully cut out the thick midribs and veins. *Thy kingdom come.* I mixed the mince with spices, a cup of rice and one egg. *Thy will be done, as in heaven, so in earth.* I snuggled one leaf of cabbage into my left palm and, with my right hand, I scooped mixed mince enough to fill the little nest. *Give us day by day our daily bread.* I folded the side edges in and started rolling the leaf from my wrist toward the tips of my fingers. *And forgive us our sins; for we also forgive every one that is indebted to us.* My hands were covered in mince and brine trickled to my elbows, but the shiver had stilled. *And lead us not into temptation; but deliver us from evil.*

I carefully rolled many cabbage leaves that night, for I-don't-know-how-many hours. Only when, through the walls or from outside, from time to time, did the word '*li-ber-ta-te*' echo in the deep pit of history, I had to step back not to let tears drop into the mixture bowl. I laid the rolls on a bed of finely-diced cabbage with a cup of water in a small pot on the stove. The gas was high. I had fallen asleep on the kitchen table. The flicker had drowned into a shimmering puddle. I woke up, removed the blanket and saw a few blotches of light in the sky. There was a glitter of hope on the roof tops and skeletal trees. I opened the window and gasped. The air bloomed into my lungs. I felt it.

Down in the street, a man in a pink short-sleeved shirt just burst out from between two houses. He smothered something red, yellow and blue at his chest. His face was worried and exhausted but it had a glow about it. He glanced around cautiously then bolted. He raised his treasure above his head and flew it like a kite. It was our flag and it had a hole cut in the middle. The coat of arms, symbol of the communist regime, had been cut out. I cried. It was over.

I live in Australia now. There is a *neighbourhood watch* sign on my house and palm trees line the street. At Christmas, neighbours wrap huge red ribbons around the palm trees. Looking at them, I ask myself: *what happened to yellow and blue?* Like me, perhaps, they are lost in the pit of history.